D1426474

OPERATION IRAQ

OPERATION IRAQ

Leo Kessler

This first world edition published in Great Britain 2004 by
SEVERN HOUSE PUBLISHERS LTD of
9–15 High Street, Sutton, Surrey SM1 1DF.
This first world edition published in the USA 2005 by
SEVERN HOUSE PUBLISHERS INC of
595 Madison Avenue, New York, N.Y. 10022.

British Library Cataloguing in Publication Data

Kessler, Leo, 1926-
    Operation Iraq
    1.   World War, 1939-1945 - Campaigns - Iraq - Fiction
    2.   War stories
    I.   Title
    823.9'14 [F]

    ISBN 0-7278-6177-8

Typeset by Palimpsest Book Production Ltd.,
Polmont, Stirlingshire, Scotland.
Printed and bound in Great Britain by
MPG Books Ltd., Bodmin, Cornwall.

Author's Note

They called themselves 'The Pact of Steel'. They were Germany, Japan and Italy, and, in 1941, they dreamed up an audacious plan to take over the world. They would drive from east and west to destroy the British Empire and then the United States. Finally, Soviet Russia would fall to them, too, and the earth would belong to them, and, in particular, to Adolf Hitler, the ruler of National Socialist Germany.

In the spring of 1941, when a sudden revolt broke out in Iraq, still dominated by the British since they had taken over the mandate in that remote country after WWI, the masters of the 'Pact of Steel' decided that Iraq would be the place where Japan and Germany would join hands and commence this march to world domination.

Thus it was that a handful of Britons fought a crucial battle against the rabidly anti-British Iraqis, who heavily outnumbered them, plus the elite of the German Army, SS Assault Battalion 'Wotan'. The British won and the Empire was saved – for a while. Now there are no more empires – 'all that red on the map' – to be saved. Still British soldiers fight and die in that cursed land of Iraq. Then, as now, the battle was – and is – one of treachery and counter-treachery, deceit upon deceit, double-dealing, cruelty and red blood. It wasn't a pleasant story. But then, in those dark days when Britain was fighting for its very life, there were no pleasant stories. Today it is no different . . .

Leo Kessler

PREFACE

The Orient Plot

'*Still gestanden!*' As one, the polished jackboots of the black-clad giants smashed down on the concrete, and the young officer with the haughty face typical of the Black Guard raised his gleaming sabre in salute.

A little officer, dwarfed by this giant in black, smiled softly. He knew, to these Germans, he, with his yellow face, small stature and trailing samurai sword, didn't look impressive. Indeed, up to the previous year or so, till Imperial Japan had begun marching westwards, conquering all before it, these same Nazi soldiers who were saluting him now would have regarded him as another 'yellow ape', a member of a non-Aryan inferior race. Now all was different, and he and the rest of his fellow Japanese were regarded as 'honorary Aryans', full partners in the 'Pact of Steel' with Germany and Italy.

Still, the little Japanese general's slant-eyed face revealed nothing of his true feelings as he inspected the guard of honour. Grasping his curved sword, cap set squarely on his shaven, bullet-head, he gazed up at the impassive faces of the 'Hitler Bodyguard Regiment' as if he might fault their turnout at any moment.

The undersized Japanese didn't. Baron Oshima, the new ambassador to Berlin, had been a regular soldier for most of his life. All the same, he was now a diplomat who was schooled in the strange ways of the Europeans, especially the Germans, whose language he spoke well. He wanted to impress the Germans, gain their support, even the friendship of their leader, Adolf Hitler. For their support was vital to the success of the Mikado's plans for world power. So, he failed to criticize. Instead he waited for the young guard commander to finish the inspection and raise his sword in salute, so that he could say in his best German, '*Gut gemacht, Sturmbannführer. Frei bier für Ihre Soldaten . . . Danke.*' The free beer did it. The officer actually flushed and, above them, waiting on the steps of his mountain retreat, Adolf Hitler smiled. He was proud of his Black Guards, the elite of the elite.

Smiling still, the Nazi leader seized the little Japanese's white-gloved hand in both of his and pressed it warmly. '*Mein lieber Herr Baron . . .*' Hitler gushed. '*Willkommen in meinem Hause.*'

A little embarrassed at such un-Japanese enthusiasm, Oshima managed to extricate his hand from Hitler's grasp and saluted, as a soldier should. 'I am honoured, *mein Führer,*' he said in his best German as the first stray flecks of the new snowfall started to drift down from the Watzmann mountain, the second highest in Germany.

Again Hitler smiled winningly. 'But my dear Baron, let us go inside, away from this snow. I must look after my guests, especially one who means so much to me and my people.'

Oshima gave a sharp intake of breath through his nose, the traditional Japanese way of showing respect, and allowed himself to be led into the Bavarian mountain home of the German leader by Hitler himself.

Already Hitler's military staff was lined up waiting to be presented to Oshima and hear, as Hitler now announced, 'Our dear friend's proposal for German-Japanese co-operation to bring about the downfall of the British Empire.'

But if that sudden announcement wasn't startling enough, Oshima's exposé of the Japanese plan, five minutes later in the villa's map room, was even more so. With the snowflakes beating the picture window with ever increasing fury, as if some God on high was attempting to destroy the war-torn world below, Oshima detailed the Japanese proposal, drawn up by the Japanese military dictator Tojo and no less a person than the Emperor himself.

Dramatically for him, Oshima slapped the great map of the world with his hard yellow hand and, with his fingers outstretched, as if he was grabbing for the whole globe, he barked, '*Ours!*'

Hitler frowned and looked at the Japanese interpreter who was standing by as if he doubted he had heard the word correctly. Next to him, his chief of staff, wooden-faced Field Marshal Keitel, looked down at the little Japanese and said gruffly, '*Herr Baron*, what do you mean – *ours?*'

Blondi, Hitler's Alsatian dog, put her tail between her legs and crept into a corner, as if she sensed that trouble lay ahead.

Oshima's face remained impassive, his dark eyes revealing nothing, as if he had not noticed the reaction to his bold statement.

'*Mein Führer*, gentlemen,' he said carefully now, realizing he had to convince these arrogant Germans he had to be taken seriously. 'Working together as we are now, Germany, Italy, of course, and Japan are now in a position to rule the world. In a matter of months, as we estimate in Tokyo, we can defeat all our enemies, both in the West and in the East.' He cast Hitler a quick glance, for Baron Oshima already knew from his spies in Berlin that Germany would attack Russia in less than six weeks, once the *Wehrmacht* had wound up its campaign in the Balkans.

Hitler's puzzled frown of a few moments before had now changed to a look of delight. It was clear to Oshima that he was telling Hitler something that he liked, though his assembled staff officers still showed their disdain for what they thought of as an inferior little yellow man who had no understanding of strategic concepts.

'With our German – and Italian – comrades advancing from the west out of Middle Europe, and the glorious Japanese Imperial Army –' again he made that strange intake of breath which indicated respect – 'from the east, together we can throw a band of steel from India, here –' he slapped the map once more – 'to the Balkans, here, which are already in German hands. Thus Russia will be cut off. As for the British in North Africa, they will be cut off from their supplies and fresh manpower in India. Their oil too. In short, the British will wither away like the grape on a vine deprived of water. As for the only other power of some importance, the United States of America –' for once Baron Oshima's face showed some emotion: it was one of contempt at the mention of the hated USA – 'we Japanese will take care of that decadent nation very shortly.' Oshima turned his gaze on Hitler once more and concluded with, 'Plan Orient, as we Japanese call it, *mein Führer*, will undoubtedly ensure that the world will be ours before this year of 1941 is over.' He dropped his right hand to his samurai sword, as if he were ready to engage anyone who might be tempted to disagree with him at that moment.

But no one was, not even the wooden-faced chief of staff Keitel. Perhaps he was silenced by the sheer bravura of the little Japanese ambassador. For a few moments a heavy brooding silence fell over the room, broken only by the beating of snowflakes against the window. All of them, participants in a conference that might change the future of the whole world, seemed wrapped up in a cocoon of their own thoughts. For even Hitler in his wildest moments had never proposed anything as radical and far-reaching as this little Japanese with his 'Plan Orient'.

Finally Keitel broke the heavy silence with, 'But the distance between the leading elements of the Japanese Army, *Herr Baron*, and our own troops in the Balkans must be at least some eight thousand kilometres. A tremendous distance. Even Alexander the Great, if I remember my ancient history correctly, was finally ruined by trying to cover the same distance, and he took years to do so.'

Oshima was ready for the question. 'Your Alexander the Great did not have aeroplanes, did he?' he said simply.

Keitel flushed. 'Wars are not won by aeroplanes,' he rasped. 'Not even in 1941.'

Hastily Hitler intervened. 'Gentlemen, let us not get down to particulars yet. Particulars always destroy brilliant, grandiose ideas. I know it well.' He looked hard at the tall, arrogant field marshal, as if accusing him of being one of those who had always poured cold water over his own 'brilliant, grandiose ideas'.

'My dear Baron,' he continued, 'I welcome such a sweeping plan. I can see how a major concerted effort, as you have suggested, would undoubtedly break the power of our enemies swiftly. But there are several imponderables which spring to mind immediately.' He let his words sink in before adding, 'The tremendous distance between our two forces, which Field Marshal Keitel has just mentioned, is naturally one of them. Another is how we can lend support to what forces we might send to bridge these distances. Our numbers would be limited and our supply lines would be stretched to the utmost. How long could we keep up the pressure against the might of the British Empire, our major enemy in the area you have mentioned, under such circumstances?'

The German staff nodded their approval and looked expectantly at the little yellow man at the centre of the discussions, as if they expected him to fall flat on his slant-eyed face, unable to come up with an answer.

Oshima surprised them. He had his answer at the ready, for he had been long prepared to have this overwhelming question put to him; indeed, he had been expecting it ever since his final interview with the Emperor, who, in his divine and infinite wisdom, had warned him that the 'round-eyed, arrogant foreign devils' would try to make a fool of him.

'Gentlemen,' he answered quite calmly, 'we in Japan have long had the experience of other nations doing our work, both politically and militarily, for us, ever since we first engaged ourselves in China back in the twenties. Everywhere in the Far East there are nations and peoples who want to free themselves from the yoke of the foreign imperialists – the French, the Dutch, the English, cost what it may. In this last decade or so, we have supported them, and in doing so, we have earned their respect and they have become the greatest supporters of Japan's imperial destiny.' Again he gave that same intake of breath, implying respect, and this time even bowed slightly. 'Soon, gentlemen, Japan's Co-Prosperity Sphere will extend throughout Asia, from Korea to Singapore.'

Hitler was impressed, though at the same time a little uneasy. He wasn't prepared to destroy the European empires in the

Far East to have them replaced by that of Japan's Co-Prosperity Sphere. But he kept his thoughts to himself and listened attentively to what the Baron had to say further on the subject.

'Now, although the situation in the Middle East is somewhat different from that in our own area,' Oshima continued, 'there are certain similarities. Again we are dealing with the two main colonial powers, Britain and France, and their territories, taken away by force from the natives back in the last century and the early twentieth century.'

Hitler cleared his throat urgently. It indicated that he didn't want a lecture on the history of the Middle East. He wanted the facts relevant to the present-day situation.

Oshima got the point. He said, 'To shorten the matter, there are today throughout the Middle East, and especially in the area we are considering for joint military operations leading to a link-up of our forces, several subject nations which would be only too eager to throw in their lot with the forces of the Pact of Steel if we could assure them they'd have national freedom.' He grinned suddenly and it wasn't a pleasant sight. 'Which, of course, we won't give them in the end. Persia, Syria, Iraq etc etc. Get those countries on our side and we won't have to worry unduly about supplies and armed men. They will do, if I may use the phrase, our dirty work for us.'

Hitler liked that. He opened his mouth to congratulate the little yellow man on his deviousness, which was worthy of the German. But before he could do so, Baron Oshima cried, throwing up both his arms in the traditional Japanese manner, '*If nothing else, gentlemen, we will bring about the destruction of the cruel, proud British Empire! Banzai . . . Banzai . . . Banzai!*'

Outside, the snowflakes pelted the window with ever-increasing fury, as if Nature itself were applauding the elemental fervour of that primeval cry. Hitler shuddered.

BOOK ONE

Revolt in the Desert

One

The sun slashed the cockney corporal's eyes like the blade of a sharp knife. To his front the scrub desert shimmered a light blue. As he and the flight sergeant squatted there in the turret of the pre-war armoured car, their shirts turned a wet black with the intense heat. Flies were everywhere. Automatically they brushed them off but they knew, from their years in Iraq, the flies would be back. They always were. As the little corporal was wont to moan, 'Give the frigging place back to the wogs.'

But now he and the balding RAF flight sergeant were too interested in the file of soldiers slogging their way through the sand and scrub towards them to notice the insects. The flight sergeant had even nearly forgotten the 'Mespot'* he'd received from his wife back in the UK, to tell him, as wives of the Iraq garrison always did, that she had 'found someone else'. He focused his glasses and tried to make out the details of those dark-skinned soldiers advancing upon the hidden armoured car.

'They're not Iraqis,' the balding flight sergeant said after a while, the sweat dripping down his brick-red face.

'Well, they're some kind of wogs,' the corporal objected. 'Only wogs and poor sods like ourselves would be out in the desert at this time of the sodding day.'

The flight sergeant grunted something and adjusted his glasses more accurately. The leading soldier came into focus more clearly now. He wore a turban like some of the Iraqi

---

* *Mespot.* Mesopotamia, old name for Iraq. Hence the name for the letter telling long-service soldiers and airmen there that their wives had deserted them.

11

levies did, and he carried a pre-war Lee Enfield rifle, but there was something about the man's bearing which distinguished him from the sloppy, ill-trained Iraqi levies in British service. It was his pack. It was squared off and well-balanced, the brasses gleaming in the harsh rays of the midday sun. Slowly he lowered his glasses, his fat face puzzled. 'Corp,' he said hesitantly. 'That lot seems to be Indian Army.'

'Indian Army?' the cockney NCO echoed. 'But there ain't no Indian Army in Iraq, just us poor sods from the frigging RAF and a handful of brown jobs back at HQ. Besides, what's those blokes doing out here in the middle of nowhere?' He indicated the featureless barren desert with a wave of his bronzed arm. 'There's nothing going on here. I mean, where they come from and where they frigging going to, I ask yer, Flight?'

For the first time that day since they had set out from the great RAF base at Habbaniyah, west of Baghdad, the fat flight sergeant forgot his unfaithful wife back in the UK, and the image of her naked in some other bloke's arms while he rogered her, going at her like a bloody fiddler's elbow. 'Yer right, Corp,' he said after a moment. 'There's something fishy going on here.'

'Yer can say that again, Flight,' the little cockney agreed. 'Take a gander at the machine gun that wog in the second file is carrying. If me glassy orbs don't deceive me, Flight, that bloke's carrying a Jerry machine gun. It ain't no Bren, for certain.' He turned to the puzzled senior NCO. 'Now tell me what a bunch of sepoys is doing in the middle of nowhere, carrying a Jerry machine gun, eh?'

But the flight sergeant had no ready answer for that overwhelming question. Instead he said, voice suddenly unsteady, 'I think, Corp, we ought to hoof it back to the armoured car. I don't like this, I don't like it one bit.'

'I ain't exactly fallen in love with it,' he agreed. 'You're right, Flight. Let's bugger off before they spot us.'

'Better get in wireless contact with base, too, while we're at it,' the flight sergeant said. 'We'd better do this proper, Corp.'

'Right you are. Blind 'em with bullshit, eh?' His bronzed face cracked into a momentary smile. 'You can do the hard graft, Flight, and wind up the elastic.'

The flight sergeant nodded. As the corporal slipped on the earphones of the armoured car's primitive wireless set, he dropped over the side of the vehicle, which it was rumoured at base had once seen service with Lawrence of Arabia back in the Old War. Even as he did so, he undid the flap of his revolver holster – just in case.

Now the column of marching men were some couple of hundred yards away. But as yet it was obvious they had not seen the armoured car. The sun was in their eyes and the vintage fighting vehicle was camouflaged to merge into the yellow waste all around. The flight sergeant spat on his palms and then seized the car's starting handle. Inside the turret, the corporal seated at the radio was commencing the usual service wireless litany. '*Charlie, Able, Baker . . . Charlie, Able, Baker . . . Are you receiving me? I repeat . . . Charlie, Able, Baker, are you receiving me . . . ? Over . . .*'

He flexed his muscles and tugged hard at the handle. There was a hollow groan. He cursed. As usual the ancient vehicles refused to start. They were clapped out like all the RAF equipment in Iraq. The government in London had ruled the rebellious Iraqis for over a quarter of a century on the cheap, using obsolete aircraft and armoured cars to keep the tribes under control, bombing them and sometimes gassing them into submission when they had been too troublesome. It had been cheaper that way, instead of using properly trained British infantry.

The flight sergeant, his fat face already lathered with sweat, as if it had been greased in vaseline, tried again. The groan turned into a whine. To his ears, it sounded as if it could be heard all the way to Baghdad. Still the advancing column of what appeared to be Indian Army soldiers didn't seem to hear. They plodded on in their files, eyes concentrated on the way ahead.

The NCO threw caution to the wind. With all his strength he turned and turned the starting handle. It was almost as if he were winding up the elastic of the toy motors he had played with as a kid. Inside the turret, the corporal was still trying to raise the big base at Habbaniyah.

It had to happen and it did. The leading Indian soldier, if that was what he was, turned in the direction of the ancient armoured car. For a moment it seemed he was unable to take in what he saw there. Suddenly he shouted, unslung his Lee Enfield and dropped to one knee in one swift movement. A second later the rest of the files were doing the same, and the sweating flight sergeant realized abruptly that he was in for trouble.

Desperately, the beads of sweat hanging like opaque pearls from his balding forehead, he turned the handle with all his strength. The whirr was now followed by a harsh wheezing. From the exhaust there came a series of gasps. The desert air was suddenly full of the cloying stink of petrol. Inside the turret, the corporal had given up trying to raise the base. For he had spotted there was danger imminent. Instead he grabbed hold of the twin handles of the armoured car's only weapon, the pre-war Vickers machine gun. He pulled back the firing slot and peered through the sights.

Two hundred yards away, the strangers were preparing to fire, and he could see from their firing postures that these were trained soldiers. But if they were soldiers of the British Indian Army, why would they attack an RAF armoured car? As the first volley rang out, the corporal posed a question that he would never live to answer. For already the first slugs were howling off the vehicle's thin armour, and the flight sergeant was down on both knees, blood jetting from his back in a bright red arc, mouth gaping open like that of some stranded fish. 'Bug–ger off, Corp,' he choked. Next instant he fell to the sand, dead before he hit the ground.

For a moment the little cockney was undecided. Could he abandon the flight sergeant just like that? It didn't seem right. They'd been out here in Iraq together ever since 1939 and, as flight sergeants went, the senior NCO wasn't a bad lot.

The slug that shattered the radio in a flurry of blue sparks and tiny red flames made up his mind for the corporal. The

Indians were on their feet, advancing in a skirmish line, firing expertly from the hip, confident that they had nothing to fear from the stationary armoured car. 'Bugger this for a tale of soldiers,' the corporal swore. He dropped the handles of the Vickers and slid into the driving seat, shoving home first gear as he did so, praying that he would not stall the ancient vehicle's tricky engine.

With a rusty grunt the armoured car moved out of its hiding place. The Indians, sensing that the armoured car was going to attempt to make a run for it, broke into a swift advance, yelling angrily as they did so. Sweating frantically now, knowing that he was fated to die like the flight sergeant had, if they caught up with him, the corporal eased the car up the sand slope, He started suddenly. There was the sound of heavy nailed boots clambering up the engine cowling to his rear. One of the Indians had outflanked him and had clambered on to the vehicle. He felt a cold finger of fear trace its way down his spine.

He pressed his foot down harder on the accelerator. But the car didn't respond. The ancient vehicles were sluggish in soft sand. 'Fer frigging hell's sake!' he cursed. 'Get a frigging move on, will yer!' He gritted his teeth and willed the armoured car to move more swiftly. As soon as he gathered speed, he'd attempt to do a swift turn and shake the bastard off the rear. Stubbornly the armoured car refused to give him the speed he needed, and the sound of the unseen Indian's heavy boots was getting closer.

While he steered, he freed one hand and reached for his pistol holster. He'd blast all hell out of any other Indian who attempted to clamber on to the armoured car. For now they were closing in on the slow-moving vehicle, its tyres attempting to get a grip on the loose sand. He gasped. He'd forgotten to put on his pistol belt when he and the dead sergeant had taken up their watching post earlier on. '*Shit . . . shit . . . shit . . . !*' he cursed, feeling himself overcome by a wave of sheer fear. He was defenceless and, whoever his attackers were, he was quite sure that he could expect no mercy from them if he fell into their hands: these Middle-Eastern wogs

15

never showed mercy when prisoners fell into their hands. And their prisoners didn't die swiftly either. In the past three years here in bloody Iraq, he had seen what had happened to some of his fellow RAF comrades when they had fallen into the hands of the locals: gouging out eyes and chopping off a bloke's John Thomas was only the start of the buggers' tortures.

The bullet hit him in the shoulder as if he had been whacked by a tremendous blow from a cricket bat. Red-hot pain skewered his flesh. He yelped. Above him in the open turret a dark, gleaming face, all white teeth and burning dark eyes, glowered down at him in triumph, as he fell momentarily back in the driver's seat. 'You die now, Tommy, eh?' the Indian said in accented English. 'Gildy, Corporal wallah!'

Suddenly he forgot his pain. Anger surged through his skinny body. How dare the wog bastard talk to a white man like him in that fashion? The adrenalin started pumping. Ignoring his wounded shoulder, he twisted the wheel sharply. Even in the soft sand, the armoured car responded. The Indian was caught off balance. He yelled. Next instant he tumbled inside the turret, to lie there momentarily, groaning, blood seeping from a great gash made by one of the Vickers' firing handles in his forehead.

The corporal didn't give him time to recover. He grabbed the reserve starting handle, steering the best he could with one hand. With an animal grunt, he brought it down hard across the Indian's face. The man raised his hands to protect himself. Too late! The angry, wounded NCO brought the handle down again with all his strength. Something snapped. The man's front teeth splintered. Blood welled from the Indian's broken nose, streaming down his chin, his shattered teeth gleaming like polished ivory. The corporal hit him again in the very same instant that the stray slug from the men firing outside struck him in the chest. For a moment he couldn't comprehend what had happened to him.

Then, with red and silver stars exploding in front of his eyes and a dark mist threatening to engulf him at any moment, he steered through his attackers blindly, scattering them to left and right, till, leaving them behind him, he could stay conscious no longer. His head slumped to the wheel, but his right foot remained clamped firmly to the accelerator. Thus the dead Indian and a dying corporal of the Royal Air Force disappeared into the desert, bearing with them the first indication that the destruction of the 300-year-old British Empire had commenced in this godforsaken hellhole . . .

Two

'I say, Jumbo,' the young flying officer with the little moustache, which stubbornly refused to grow into the typical RAF aircrew handlebar one, lisped. 'What's going on?' He and his companion narrowed their eyes against the glare of the midday sun after the cool darkness of the officers' mess. 'These towel-heads are making a fuss, what.'

His companion, equally young and inexperienced, said, 'Wogs and shitehouse wallahs at that. What can you expect? Wogs!' He spat out the word, as if by itself it was explanation enough.

The young flying officer from the great sprawling Habbaniyah training base was not appeased. 'Shitehouse wallahs don't run around at this time of day and in this heat,' he commented, as more and more of the natives who cleaned the camp's latrines and burned the evil-smelling ordure in large pits on the outskirts of Habbaniyah left their unpleasant tasks and ran towards what looked like an RAF armoured car which was slowly approaching the centre of the base. 'There's something going on, Jumbo.'

Behind them, Air Commodore Jeeves, erect and somewhat sour-faced, still limping from the wound he had received in the Battle of Britain the year before, frowned. That silly young fool Gore-Smythe, with his even sillier moustache, was right. The natives didn't usually go galloping about like this in the baking midday heat, where it was sometimes possible to fry an egg on the decks of the armoured cars which patrolled deep into the desert around the remote base, which the British used to control Iraq. Besides, what was the armoured car that had attracted their attention doing weaving all over the place like that? If he hadn't known better, he would have thought that the unknown driver was three sheets into the wind.

Jeeves turned to Squadron Leader McLeod, commander of the RAF armoured car squadron and an old hand in Iraq, who was just behind him, finishing off his Victory cigarette before he went over to his workshops. 'One of your cars, McLeod. D'ye think the driver's suffering from heatstroke? The bugger's all over the place.'

McLeod, nut-brown, face pared down to the bone from years in the desert and the illnesses he had suffered here since he had first come out to Iraq during the British campaign of 1920 against the unruly Iraqis, snapped, 'Bin watching him myself, sir. Does look as if he's in trouble. Want me to have a look see?'

At any other time, Jeeves would have smiled. The dour Scot was not one to waste words. He always chopped off his sentences like that. But not this April day. There was trouble – serious trouble in the air. Everywhere in the Middle East the situation was deteriorating rapidly for the British Empire. Not only in North Africa, where the Eighth Army was suffering defeat after defeat at the hands of the Huns, but also in Syria, now controlled by the French puppets of the victorious Germans. Iraq was no better. Here and in Persia, the Germans were trying to raise the tribes against the British. They had done so in the First World War, and now, with the British fighting alone and without success, it was clear that the Arabs would be only too eager to throw in their lot with the Hun and get rid of the hated *Inglizi*.

'I'll get the Norton, sir,' McLeod offered.

'And I'll come with you,' a worried Jeeves added. 'There's something ruddy wrong over there.' And then, angry at the two young flying officers still in training with his wing for some reason he couldn't quite fathom, he snapped, 'Well, the two of you, don't just stand around like a couple of pregnant penguins. Get back to your manuals. You've got one hell of a lot to learn before the balloon goes up, and I can assure you it will, sooner than you two young twerps think.' They fled.

'Oh my God!' Jeeves exclaimed, as McLeod slithered to a

stop in a curve of flying sand, sending the gawping Iraqis to one side, as they gazed at the battered armoured car, which had finally come to a stop, crashed into one of the marker beacons which indicated the end of the base's runway. But its engine was still running. Reeves thought the sound strange. Like the beating of a metal heart, although no other sound came from within the vehicle.

McLeod waved his swagger cane threateningly at the natives. They retreated even further back. They all knew the squadron leader. He was a feared man. Anyone who crossed him disappeared silently and suddenly; McLeod didn't have the normal Britisher's sense of discipline and fair play. The dour Scot was worse than their old Turkish masters, and these piercing light-blue eyes of his were supposed among them to bring evil upon anyone who gazed at them too long.

For a moment or two, the officers gazed at the stalled armoured car, its sides pocked with the silver scars of bullets, and at the dead Indian soldier sprawled along the engine cowling. Then McLeod moved. He clambered aboard, looked down at the driver slumped over his wheel, the blood congealing from his wounds and great bluebottles beginning to crawl across his pale face into the sightless eyes. He turned to the air commodore. 'Dead – the driver, I mean.'

Reeves nodded his understanding. He indicated the Indian sepoy.

'I know, sir,' the Scot said slowly and thoughtfully. 'What in hell's name is a member of the Indian Army doing here in Iraq?'

Reeves bit his bottom lip in puzzled vexation. Most of the regular Indian Army was in the Middle East fighting the Hun; the rest were on the Indian frontier with Burma, waiting for those evil little yellow men, the Japs, to attack, which undoubtedly they would do soon. There were no Indian Army troops to spare for this sideshow in Iraq. So what was the Indian doing here? Why had he been involved in what was, Reeves hazarded, an attack on the RAF armoured car patrol; and, to judge by the number of bullet holes in the car's side, Jeeves guessed there had been more than one attacker. He pushed back his forage cap and scratched the back of his shaven head. There was something funny going on here, but for the life of him, he couldn't make out what it was.

Five minutes later, when the police had arrived and cleared away the evil-smelling 'shitehouse wallahs', McLeod started to enlighten the puzzled air commodore. While the RAF police encircled the armoured car, rifles and clubs at the ready, Jeeves clambered on to the car and squatted where the Scot was examining the dead Indian. McLeod said, 'Oh yes, Commodore, he's an Indian all right. Look at the mark on his forehead. Lower caste, admittedly, but a caste mark all right. The gear's Indian Army, too. But look at this.' Relatively gently for him, McLeod turned the dead man over. 'Take a gander at his water bottle. Not British Army issue.'

Jeeves nodded. It was certainly not the type issued to the RAF as well as the British Army – the flat, square bottle, enclosed in what looked like khaki serge and holding the usual quart of water. This one was smaller, fatter and held perhaps half that quantity of water, and instead of the plug top of the British model, this had a screw, nozzle-type top. The colour was different too, not khaki, but field grey. 'So, what do you make of it, McLeod?' he asked after a moment.

The Scot didn't answer immediately. Instead he asked a question of his own. 'Strange, isn't it, sir. But here we have a member of the Indian Army appearing, apparently out of the blue, clad in British Army issue equipment, save for a German water bottle. Now, that's pretty strange, wouldn't you think, sir?'

Jeeves was angry for a moment. He didn't like people playing guessing games with him, even experts like McLeod. 'Come off it, McLeod. Don't play games with me. What are you bloody well trying to say?'

'This, sir. How did this bloke get here? I checked, while we got rid of the towel-heads, with the port authorities at Basra. There are no Indian units there. So, how did he and his mates – there were obviously others – get here?'

'Dropped in from the bloody sky, naturally,' Jeeves said ironically.

21

'Exactly, sir.'

'What?'

'You said it, sir.'

'Said what?' Jeeves demanded.

'*Dropped in from the sky.*' The Scot's pale-blue eyes displayed unusual warmth for such a serious, dour man. Hastily, before his senior officer exploded, McLeod pulled back the dead man's shirt so that the air commodore could view the skinny, delicate, brown torso below. 'Look at that, sir,' he urged.

'Look at what?'

'Those red puckered lines around the shoulders, and the slight bruise just above the dead man's belly button. Do you see them?'

'Yes, I do. But what do they signify, for God's sake? And please, McLeod, don't give me any more ruddy puzzles, I'm running out of patience. And this bloody heat isn't helping any.'

'Marks from a chute – a parachute, sir. Not so long ago, this dead bloke here came out of an aircraft attached to a piece of knickers silk. Those are the marks the harness left on him.'

Jeeves was surprised, very surprised, but he concealed it. It never did to show one's feelings to lower-ranking officers; they lost confidence in one's leadership qualities if one did. All the same, he was constrained to ask the Scot, 'Why? Why have he and his comrades been dropped by parachute here in neutral Iraq, and, for God's sake, *who* dropped them?'

McLeod had his answer ready. 'The Huns, sir. The Indian is perfectly kitted out, save for the water bottle, which is German, and if you'll look at his boots.' He pulled up the dead man's left foot and showed his superior the typical British Army ammunition boot underneath the neatly tied khaki puttees. 'Just look at the studs. They're arranged in the regulation thirteen, but they're different.'

Puzzled and surprised as he was, Jeeves had no time for further riddles. 'All right, McLeod, how are they different and what do they signify?'

'British Army studs are round, these are triangular.'

'So?'

'They're German Army issue, sir.' He didn't wait for Jeeves to react. 'This man already possessed most of his Indian Army gear, but not a water bottle. It's not the sort of thing you'd need in a POW camp. A bloke would probably sling it away immediately after he was captured—'

'You mean, this Indian wallah was once a German POW?' Jeeves interrupted the Scot harshly.

'I do. One of the thousands of Indians taken prisoner in the Western Desert, sir, once the Huns moved in and took over from the Eyeties there. Naturally, those POWs would be subjected to German pressure to make them join in the German cause. The Hun tried the same trick in World War One. Nowadays there are better reasons for them to want to help the Huns to remove our cruel –' his craggy dour face cracked into a wintry smile at the word – 'domination of their country. Gandhi and all the rest of those Indian Congress wallahs. My guess, sir, is that his nibs here was one of those Indians who succumbed to German pressure.' He let the dead man's foot go and his boot slammed hollowly against the burning metal deck of the wrecked armoured car.

For a moment or two there was silence while Jeeves stared down at the dead man in bewilderment, his mind paralysed and unable to work out what this discovery meant. Finally he said, somewhat weakly, 'Well, what do you think, McLeod? You're the old hand.'

McLeod didn't answer immediately. It was as if he, too, needed a conscious act of willpower before he could express an opinion. 'Well, sir, let's say this man and his companions might be a sort of recce. They'd fit in here well enough – their colour, religion – and they're seemingly part of the British Imperial military presence.'

'But a recce for what?' Jeeves objected.

'For the Huns.'

'But the nearest Huns are in the Middle East and in Greece. There's surely thousands of miles between them and us here, McLeod.'

The Scot had an answer to that question ready. 'I think that this recce is not meant for a full-scale assault force, sir. Perhaps the Germans will send in just enough troops – probably by air – to stiffen up Raschid Ali—'

'That greasy traitor!' Jeeves interjected scornfully. 'If anybody needs his backbone stiffening, it's that bastard up there in Baghdad, if you'll excuse my French.'

'I will, sir. But if Raschid Ali does get German support, the Iraqi generals will go over to him. Then it won't take much convincing – or *baksheesh* –' he made the Arab gesture of counting banknotes with his thumb and forefinger – 'to make the generals take part in open warfare against us. They know just how weak our forces are here in Iraq.' The Scot shrugged his skinny shoulders. 'Then we *will* be up the creek without a paddle. Cut off as we are here, it could be another Kut.'

Involuntarily Jeeves shuddered. He'd been a schoolboy at the time of the Kut massacre and what followed when the Turkish military forced the British garrison to surrender at Kut in the then Mesopotamia, but the terrible events of that time were still etched on his memory. Even today, nearly thirty years after Kut, when he was a battle-hardened commander who had seen plenty of unpleasant incidents in his time, he couldn't bring himself to remember what the Turks and their Iraqi allies had done to the thousand-odd British soldiers who had surrendered to them. The thought gave him the impetus to make a quick decision. 'All right, McLeod, I'll buy it. You are probably right. The Hun's up to his usual nasty tricks here in Iraq, and the whole business is probably linked with that greasy bastard in the capital, Raschid Ali. He'd sell his own mother for a couple of quid if it would help him to gain power. So this is what I'd like you to do, McLeod.'

'Sir?'

'How many armoured cars can you spare from your routine desert patrols?'

'Three, as long as I have nine runners to protect the base in case . . .' He didn't finish his sentence, but Jeeves knew what the Scot meant – in case the bloody balloon went up.

'All right, take a troop of three, McLeod. I'll give you forty-eight hours. Find these other Indians and bring in prisoners. It's vitally urgent we find out more about what's going on. Understood?'

'Understood, sir. I'll get right on to it as soon as I get this vehicle towed away.'

'Don't bother about it. I'll see to the towing away myself personally. At the double now.' He flashed the older squadron leader a fleeting smile. 'And the best of luck.'

McLeod, as serious as he always was, didn't return the smile. Instead he said, 'I'm off, sir.' He paused momentarily before adding, 'And watch your back, sir. You know what the Iraqis are like.' And with that he was gone, leaving Jeeves to stare at the bare yellow horizon beyond the great sprawling camp, a growing feeling of apprehension and doubt slowly beginning to seep through his body.

Three

McLeod cursed. The engine of the second armoured car was overheating already. They had been out on patrol searching for the mysterious Indians for not more than an hour and already, as usual, he was having trouble with the antiquated vehicles.

It was typical, McLeod told himself, as the crew of the second armoured car poured more water into its radiator. The British Government, in their infinite wisdom, had tried to run Iraq on a pittance. They'd used the RAF, flying obsolete planes as well, and cheap Assyrian levies, to control a big country, plagued by warring tribes and, since 1930, governed by treacherous, supposedly pro-British politicians in Baghdad, who could be bought and bribed at the drop of a hat.

Just before he had set out, minus one armoured car which refused to start for some reason, a gloomy Jeeves had confided in him that all he had to defend the great sprawling Habbaniyah Base were some 1,000 Assyrians and about the same number of RAF personnel, who were flying and servicing eighty planes, all of them of pre-war vintage. In addition, there were some 8,000 civilians, some of them British, who Jeeves said he could arm if he could find enough weapons for them.

As Jeeves confided to McLeod, looking to left and right to check whether he was being overheard (for there were spies everywhere in the camp), 'If the balloon does go up here, McLeod, and the Iraqi Army gets into the act, we'll be hopelessly outnumbered. That is, unless we get reinforcements from home or from India, which looks doubtful in view of the Eighth Army's situation in the Middle East.' He sighed and sucked at the stem of his unlit pipe (for some reason the air commodore had decided to stop smoking his beloved briar when everyone else seemed to be smoking more due to the rising tension in the desert country). *'Nil desperandum*, what, McLeod. Smile through your tears and all that bullshit, eh?' McLeod had responded with a careful smile of his own. Jeeves was doing his best. Unfortunately, old Mespot hand that he was, he knew better than the air commodore how bad the situation was in Iraq. He knew from Intelligence that they had been picking up morse signals ever since the end of March. They appeared to come from outside Iraq and, according to the Intelligence wallahs, they were strong enough to be coming from neighbouring Syria.

Syria was under the control of the Vichy French government, which was actively co-operating with the Nazis on the French mainland. As far as Intelligence was concerned, that meant the Germans were partially running the show in Syria, for the coded messages should have been easily cracked. British Intelligence had long been able to read French Army codes. So, Intelligence had concluded that the morse signals were using the German code which hadn't been deciphered so far.

McLeod watched his sweating half-naked men finish off filling up the radiator with precious water, wondering if he was going to have enough for the patrol. If he didn't, he and his men would have to sacrifice some of their own water, and they were limited to a quart a day for all purposes – drinking, washing and remaining clean-shaven in the best traditions of the Royal Air Force. It was bloody, very bloody, but it had always been that way in this godforsaken country. Sometimes he wondered why he had stayed here so long. In reality, he knew. Iraq, in some awful bloody way, was home to him. He had long forgotten what Scotland was like. As he gave the signal for his two crews to mount up, he told himself, 'Jock, old pal, they're gonna bury you in this bluidy arsehole of the universe.' Five minutes later, the two lone armoured cars were on their way again, tiny dots in that vast yellow sea of sand.

McLeod, the veteran, worked his vehicle on the grid system, covering a square of some twenty miles between the base and the main road to Baghdad. Even as he selected the route for the search, he told himself it would be highly unlikely that these mysterious Indians would be heading – at least, openly – for the Iraqi capital. As he had anticipated, he found nothing save a convoy of skinny-ribbed camels heading for God knew where, whose handlers had seen nothing. Thereafter he checked a couple of the more well-known watering holes. But although there was evidence that they had been used recently, there were no tracks or footprints of nailed Indian Army boots to indicate the Indians had been there. That evening, as he and his men squatted next to the cars, drinking strong 'sarnt-major's tea' and eating hard tack biscuits spread with corned beef that had poured out of the big tins in almost liquid form, McLeod decided on another tack.

Idly listening to the soft talk of the men, mainly concerned with 'subject number one', i.e. sex, McLeod tried to work out what would be the Indians' aim here in Iraq. If they were there to do some job for, say, the French in Syria, and that job was somehow connected with a possible revolt by the Baghdad Iraqis, he reasoned, then the Indians might well be doing a recce of the base area itself. But what would they be looking for?

'So I got her in the back of the barn,' 'Chalky' White, the big driver of number one car was saying in this thick Barnsley accent, 'and I said, "No, come on, lass, have them drawers off'n yer right now. You've had yer port and lemon and yer fish-and-tatie supper. Yer can't expect me to pay that kind of money on yer without a bit o' slap and tickle in return." '

McLeod gave a little smile. Soldiers never changed, he told himself. They were talking the same kind of stuff about their 'bints, booze and baccy' when he had first come out here a green young officer of the Royal Flying Corps in what seemed now another age. Thank God they never did change. Who back home would accept this kind of life, with all its hardships, if they weren't a regular?

'So yer knows what she sez to me, muckers?' Chalky was saying. ' "I got more than fish and taties from that flight sergeant last week. He gave me a proper sitdown knife-and-fork supper an' a gin and tonic. Now, he was a real gent. Knew how to treat a lady. He even took my drawers off for me . . ."'

McLeod forgot 'Chalky' White's sexual memoirs and concentrated once again on the problem at hand. If these mysterious Indians *were* doing a recce for either the Iraqis or some other power and they were paying special attention to the Habbaniyah Base, they'd obviously look for suitable spots for artillery, or places where the infantry could mass in dead ground safe from British fire or aerial attack. It seemed to him, therefore, that the best place for an assault to be initiated would be in the low foothills east of the camp, between it and the main road to Baghdad. Those hills would be additionally well located close to the motor road, for bringing up further enemy troops if necessary. The more he thought about it, the better McLeod liked the idea. But there was one catch. The cars' radio sets, again damnably old, were pretty useless at the best of times. In the foothills, however, they would be more than useless. Their transmissions wouldn't carry more than a mile or so. If he ran into trouble out there, there'd be no chance of contacting base. They'd be on their own and he could guess what would happen to them then. They wouldn't be coming back – or, if they did, it would be in a wooden box . . .

At dawn, McLeod had his little force on the move again. He and his crews savoured the dawn coolness, hardly noticing the roughness of the terrain, the potholes and ruts of the track, which made the springs of the ancient armoured cars squeak alarmingly. Standing upright in the turret of the lead car, muffled up in his sheepskin coat and wearing motoring goggles, for it was damnably cold and the bitter wind threw razor-sharp sand particles at his red-raw face, McLeod surveyed the way ahead for any sign of life. But there was none. They might well have been the last men left alive on earth.

The hours passed leadenly. Now, in the blue haze of the distance, with the sun already high in the sky, McLeod could see his objective – the brown smudge of the foothills. Carefully he scanned it with his binoculars. He was searching for any sign of life – a hut or spiral of smoke which might indicate a cooking fire. But there was none. The foothills appeared deserted and void of human life, save for the skeletons of camels and other livestock, dead these many years.

All the same, McLeod felt in his lean guts that he was on the right track. He had to be, he told himself, for his fuel and water were running out. Tomorrow he'd have to return to base, unless he wanted to walk back, and that could lead to his own bones joining the other white-bleached bones that littered the desert floor.

It was dark when they reached the foothills, and the men were exhausted, parched and red-eyed with the strain of driving for so many hours. Although he didn't like to stop now, McLeod knew he had to; the men needed a rest. Indeed, the men were too hungry to open their tins of sausage and Canadian bacon wrapped in greaseproof paper and cook them. So McLeod, the good commander, sprang a surprise on them. He produced the six big cans of Syrian peaches which he had bribed the cooks into giving them and handed them over to Chalky White to distribute among the suddenly delighted crews.

For a while, McLeod slept heavily, as did the others snoring heartily, save for the sentry, who was trying to keep warm in McLeod's sheepskin coat. But about three, just after the sentries had changed, he woke with a start. For a moment or two, he wondered what had wakened him. Propping his head up under his blanket, he stared at the night sky, bright with the silver light of a myriad cold stars, listening to the 'singing of the sand', as the old Iraq hands called it. At night the grains of sand contracted in the bitter cold, then they rubbed together, for some reason, giving off a strange haunting sound.

But after a few moments of listening, he realized it wasn't the 'singing of the sand' which had wakened him. It was another sound altogether.

This one was higher, shriller, more urgent than the gentle, almost magical music of the shifting night sands. This was a mechanical, busy sound. Immediately McLeod was fully awake. He wasted no time. He shrugged off his blankets, feeling no cold now in the urgency of the movement.

Tugging out his revolver, he hurried in a crouch to where the sentry, Chalky White, stood motionless, head cocked to one side as if he were listening too. 'Do you hear it, Leading Aircraftsman?'

White nodded and answered in a voice that was subdued, for him, 'Ay, I did that, sir.'

'Morse?'

'Sounds like it to yours truly, sir.'

McLeod frowned, puzzled, but before he could ask the question he was about to pose, White did it for him. 'Who the hell can be sending morse at this time o' night in the middle of the bleeding desert, sir?'

Now McLeod had his answer ready. 'The Indians, I suspect, White. Who else, eh?'

'Well, let's go and get the buggers,' the aircraftsman answered, grasping his rifle more tightly and preparing to rise, face set and hard in the silver light of the stars.

McLeod grabbed him hastily. 'Let's take it easy, White. We don't want to go at it like a bull at a gate. We want to take some of them, at least, alive, and we can only do that if we don't engage in a shooting match. Besides, for all we know, they might outnumber us.'

White spat drily into the sand. 'Ay, sir, but they's darkies and we're white, ain't we? Besides, sir, we've got the two Vickers in the armoured cars.' But McLeod wasn't listening. For he was already working out a plan of attack and it didn't include waking up half the countryside with the racket that the ancient armoured cars would make starting up. His RAF crewmen would complain. But there was no other way. They'd have to go in on foot, catching the Indians, if it was the Indians, by surprise. And the best time to do that was just before dawn, when the enemy would be still huddled in their blankets catching a last few minutes of sleep before yet another day in that harsh sun commenced. There was only one catch, he told himself. Whoever was sending that morse might well be awake at dawn and give the alarm. But that was a chance McLeod was prepared to take. Suddenly he felt happy. It was like the times when he had been a young man, eager, in that silly way of young officers, to get into action. He smiled to himself and then started to give White his orders . . .

Four

Commandant Lestrade slumped in the easy chair, legs apart, flies open, and watched the plump Syrian girl, one of the many he ordered from the Damascus red-light district when he was on night duty and there were none of the damned Boche officers around, tut-tutting about lax morals like a lot of damned old maids. In the next room, the operators were still taking the morse messages from the infiltrators. It was his job to ensure security was watertight and report anything urgent to the Germans of the so-called 'control commission', which, in reality, was a cover for the new masters of French Syria.

Not that he had minded. He had been working secretly for the Boche and other fascist organizations since 1938. Back before the war, he had reported to the right-wing French Calougards; then, when he had been posted to the Maginot Line a year later, he had transferred his allegiance totally to the Germans, betraying to them what he knew of the French fortifications in the Metz-Montmedy area. They had paid him well, especially after the *Wehrmacht* had been able to break through so easily in that area thanks, in part, to his information. After their victory, there had been little for him to do to earn enough francs to pay for the perverted girls he liked, and the rest of what he called his 'little luxuries'. A major's pay meant nothing, especially now that the franc had been effectively devalued.

It had been for this reason that he had jumped at the chance of a posting to Syria to replace an officer who had refused to pledge his loyalty to Vichy France, and had defected to the English swine to join that gawky traitor General de Gaulle.

Naturally the Boche had contacted him almost as soon as he had arrived in the French colony. They were well-organized swine. Still, their money was good and it meant that he could afford a regular supply of young Syrian whores and the like, who could perform for him during these long nights when he was on duty at this secret listening post.

Now, while the morse buzzed in the next room, he fondled his flaccid penis, his red, pig-like eyes glistening as he watched the whore's every move, giving her instructions every now and again on how to excite him even more, though he was finding it increasingly difficult to get the satisfaction he sought. 'Do it more slowly,' he commanded, as the naked whore gyrated in front of him, her dark body sweating as if she were smeared with vaseline. 'You know how long it takes me to get really excited.' He pulled hopefully at his organ. Nothing! He cursed and gazed at the woman once more, licking his thick red sensualist's lips as he did so.

Outside, a section of the Foreign Legion were marching by. Once they had chanted the slow march of the Legion, the *'Boudin'*, when they had marched. Now they sang one of those damned Boche marching songs, *'Oh, du schöner Westerwald'* or something like that. Naturally the Boche commission in Damascus had cultivated the Legion; half of the soldiers were German anyway. They'd be useful in the great battle to come, Lestrade told himself.

For a moment he forgot the naked girl attempting to seduce him. He didn't know the Boches' plan, of course. He was just a minor cog in the machinery, he realized that. But whatever it was, it was big, very big. Why else were these Indians out there in the desert on the other side of the Syrian border? They had some sort of important role in whatever was planned. They had to be important. Why else would the Boche pay him good money to record their messages and pass them on to the German commission here in Damascus? They would have been forced to bribe Colonel Joubert of the French *Deuxième Bureau* too, so that he, Lestrade, could use this facility – and it took money, big money, to bribe the head of the French secret service.

The whore had opened her legs wider now, revealing the

black line of pubic hair and the faint pink behind it. He caught his breath. She was exciting him now. He already felt a slight tumescence in his flabby loins. 'Agitate it,' he ordered. 'Play with it. That is really exciting.'

'*Oui, mon Commandant*,' she said obediently. She wet her middle finger and brushed it lightly between her legs. She pretended to shiver, as if with sexual pleasure.

'Good, good!' he choked, fat face turning red with excitement now, his lips suddenly dry. He pressed his penis more strongly. 'You shall have it soon,' he choked. 'But you must wait till my great thing is ready to penetrate you. Then you'll scream, you damned little slut.'

'Yes,' she breathed in feigned ecstasy, moving her middle finger up and down more rapidly, as if she could barely contain her passion. Under her breath she whispered contemptuously, '*Sale con.*'

'You can do it faster now,' he called huskily. 'I'm . . . getting there. Faster!' He touched his ugly member with his fat paw proudly, as if he had achieved something of great significance.

She did as he wished, groaning a little, her eyes half-closed. The sooner she got it over with, the better, she told herself. 'How you torment me,' she sighed, her mouth suddenly slack, as if she had been transported by overwhelming passion into a sexual world of her own.

His piggy eyes flashed greedily, taking in every detail of her writhing dark body. 'You're enjoying it, aren't you?' he gasped throatily. 'I wager you do it all the time . . . when I'm not here.' He groaned. 'Just waiting . . . till I can pleasure you down there with my great thing.'

'Yes . . . yes!' she cried, twisting her head from side to side, her long hair swinging wildly with the movement of her body. 'You must do it to me . . . I can't wait . . . please, I beg you . . . do it to me . . . *Now!*' The plea seemed to explode from her wet gaping mouth.

'Hold it . . . hold it . . . I shall do it,' he gasped, pulling mightily at his penis, his face glazed with sweat, his face brick-red, as if he might have a stroke at any moment.

She risked a quick look at him, as he writhed in his chair. His fat body was trembling with lust as he tugged mightily at his organ. '*Cochon!*' she cursed to herself. 'How much longer.' At that moment she wished she weren't here. Why didn't the bastard have a stroke and get it over with? Even the *Unteroffizier* from the Boche control commission, whom she 'serviced' every Saturday afternoon after he had received his pay, was better than this swine of a fellow countryman. He didn't make all this fuss. He paid his money, let her wash his loins and put on the stout German contraceptive, trade mark '*Vulkan*'*, and then got on with it. Afterwards he left her a little present, saluted her for some reason, and said, in the few words of French he spoke, '*À bientot,*' then departed.

'*Allez . . . allez,*' he alerted her to her duties. 'I am ready now. Come on top of it before it goes down . . . I shall give it to you . . . *Vite!*'

'*Je viens,*' she responded, stopping playing with herself. She was already hurting down there as it was.

'Hurry, I'll give you it.'

But *Commandant* Lestrade was not fated to give the Syrian whore 'it' this night, or any other night for that matter. In the next room, the frantic buzz of morse had ceased abruptly. Then, while the whore positioned herself above the the gasping officer, his eyes screwed tightly shut as if he wished to blot out everything but his sexual fantasies, his pudgy hands feeling for her hips blindly, there was a sudden urgent hammering on the door of his little office, and an alarmed voice was crying, '*Mon Commandant . . . Commandant: . . . nous avons un problème . . . la transmission d'Irak . . .* the transmission is broken . . .'

He was waiting for her outside the *Café de la Legion*, kepi tilted rakishly to one side of his shaven head, woollen scarf thrown carelessly about his neck, cheap cigarette glued to the side of his mouth. She gave her tight little whore's smile. Her contact was doing his Jean Gabin act again. Still, 'Jo-Jo', as she called him, didn't demand anything from her but information, for which he paid; and, for some reason, she felt, he

* Volcano.

36

wasn't one of those turncoats and traitors who seemed to fill Damascus these days.

Jo-Jo shook her hand and then embraced her in the French fashion, though somehow she didn't think he was French, despite his fluent knowledge of the language, and the French style which he cultivated. 'A drink?' he asked. 'We've still got time before the curfew.'

She shook her head. 'I drink too much already.'

He nodded his understanding. '*Bon.* What news from the fat *commandant* of the teleprinters? Did you get anything out of him –' he hesitated momentarily – 'er – afterwards?'

She wondered at that 'afterwards' and the pause before it. Frenchmen, especially soldiers, weren't usually so sensitive. Was he a Boche? There were plenty of them in the Legion. She dismissed the idea. The Boche might be respectful, but they weren't modest in the matter of sex. Was he perhaps a *Rosbif*? Before she had time to answer that question to herself, he said: 'Two *flics*!'

She knew what to do immediately. Neither of them wanted the two gendarmes sauntering down the darkened avenue, swinging their white clubs, to stop and question them, perhaps even ask for their papers. She swept into his arms, as they came closer, chatting softly to one another, that is, if '*flics*' could ever talk softly.

Jo-Jo, if that was his real name, also knew the drill. He put his arms around her and whispered into her ear, 'I'll show 'em your arse. The *flics* always like to see a piece of rump flesh. Satisfies the pig in them.'

She giggled and felt his big hand on her backside. She wasn't wearing knickers. She never did when she was working. Some pervert or so would have surely stolen them. The *flics* came closer. Jo-Jo worked his lower body closer to hers, as if he were already slipping it to her. She felt him raise her skirt even higher, so that the two cops could get an eyeful.

They did. One of them laughed coarsely and commented, 'You've got it in the wrong place, sonny,' and then, swinging their clubs, they passed on without any further comment.

Jo-Jo released her when they had turned the corner. She said, 'Did you like that, Jo-Jo? And it didn't cost you anything.'

'Yes. Of course. Many thanks.'

She realized he had no interest in her sexual charms, though she could tell from his reaction as he had pressed close to her a moment before that he was straight. He said, 'Anything then?'

Swiftly she told him what had transpired, just as the fat swine had been about to finish his piggery, and how his anger had changed to anxiety when the clerk had told him what had happened in the radio room. He hadn't even slapped her and blamed it all on her, as was often the case when she couldn't get him sexually aroused, or when anything else had gone wrong; he had been too concerned to get the information, whatever it was, to his German masters.

Jo-Jo listened attentively to what she had to say.

When she had finished, he asked, 'And you're sure that the clerk said from Iraq? It's important, you know.'

She didn't know, but all the same she nodded and assured him that was what the clerk had said.

For a moment, the two of them stood there in the gloom of the 'dim-out' while Jo-Jo obviously considered what she had said. Then, as the siren started to sound the approach of the nightly curfew for Damascus, he reached into his wallet and handed her the usual payment before saying, 'Thank you for your help, *chérie*. You are a good girl.' He tapped her pert rump playfully and, for a moment, she was tempted to ask him to come home with her and dance the mattress polka for free. But then she saw he was anxious to be on his way, though before he did so, he surprised her. Setting his white kepi at the regulation angle, just in case he met the military police on his way to the barracks, if that was where he was going now, he reached forward and pressed his lips against hers. She was caught completely by surprise. For when had even a common soldier kissed a whore? But before she could recover and ask him if he were suffering from the *cafard* or some other brain disease, he was gone with a murmured '*au revoir, chérie*', to disappear into the gloom . . .

38

Five

McLeod's little group of RAF men had come in on both flanks. The going had been tough, made tougher by the darkness. They had encountered a ridge on the left flank and had been forced to climb it. Digging their toes into the soft rock and sand, they had edged their way up it, fighting the sharp-bladed grass and camel thorn which ripped and tore at their uniforms and flesh cruelly.

McLeod was fit, but he was twice as old as his men and within seconds he was panting hard, desperately trying not to cry out when the thorn ripped his arms. Once he slipped and ripped off a nail. Red-hot agonizing pain shot through his body and he had to bite his bottom lip till the blood came to suppress a cry.

But in the end they made it and peered down at the little encampment. As McLeod had guessed, the Indians were enjoying the last minutes of their sleep before the dawn came, and the sole sentry was slumped in front of a flickering fire of camel thorn and dung, rifle resting between his skinny brown knees, a blanket thrown over his shoulders. It was obvious that the Indians anticipated no danger.

Still, McLeod, the old hand, was careful. As the rest of his group came in from the other flank, he surveyed the ground for any sign of enemy precautions – empty ration tins filled with pebbles dangling from wire, sharpened wooden stakes set at an angle in holes and the like. But there appeared to be none.

Slowly the squadron leader raised his clumsy-looking flare pistol. With it he would signal his two groups to attack, and at the same time signal the two men guarding the armoured cars that they were going in. He didn't want the two men some two hundred yards to the rear to get jumpy when the firing commenced.

He had curled his finger around the trigger, knowing, as he did on all such occasions, that by doing so he might start something in which good men could be killed. Then he dismissed the thought and took final pressure. The pistol barked. There had been a slithering hiss. Smoke ejected from the big brass muzzle. The flare shot into the pre-dawn sky. A second went by. Another. Below, in the little camp, nothing stirred. The bark of the Verey pistol had not even alerted the sentry swathed in his blanket at the camp fire.

A crack. Sharp like a bone-dry twig snapping underfoot in a summer forest. The Verey flare burst into a blossom of glowing incandescent green. Suddenly, startlingly, all hell had broken loose. From the flanks, the two groups of RAF men had started to advance, firing from the hip as they did so. At the fire, the Indian sentry threw off his blanket. Frantically he had grabbed for his rifle. Too late. Mcleod rose and, tossing aside his Verey pistol, fired his .38. At that range he could not have missed. The Indian shrieked with agony. He threw up his skinny brown arms like someone attempting to climb the rungs of an invisible ladder. But there was no escaping Death. He staggered. Next moment he slammed face forward into the wood fire. Abruptly the air was full of the sickening stench of burning human flesh.

Now a wild fire fight had broken out. Like men advancing against a gale, crouched low and firing from the hip, the attackers advanced. An RAF man cursed. He went down clutching his shattered knee, crying obscenities. Still the others came on, firing into the Indians, who, trained soldiers as they were, were milling around in confusion, as if they didn't know what to do next.

In truth they had little choice but to stand and fight it out. The RAF men had them trapped; and now they were enjoying that feeling that they were in charge. Perhaps it was an outlet for their frustrations at being stationed in this arse of the world, with its heat, flies, sickness and the lack of women.

Now they took almost sadistic pleasure in gunning the trapped Indians down without mercy. Twice McLeod thought he heard someone shout in English. 'Cease firing *please* . . . No shoot!' But the attackers took no notice. Neither did they when McLeod himself bellowed. 'I want prisoners, men . . . For Chrissake, don't shoot all of 'em. I need prisoners . . .' The unreasoning lust of battle had taken over, that atavistic desire to kill and kill again. Undoubtedly they would have slaughtered the Indians to the last man but for the sudden flight of flares to the rear, where the two RAF men guarded the armoured car, followed a moment later by an urgent burst of Vickers fire.

'Shit!' McLeod exclaimed, knowing instinctively that something had gone wrong. The flares signalled immediate return to base. More importantly, the burst of machine-gun fire indicated that the cars themselves seemed to be under attack. Abruptly his carefully planned attack on the unsuspecting Indians had gone horribly wrong.

McLeod hesitated no longer. He cupped his hands about his mouth and bellowed above the angry snap and crack of the small arms battle, 'Pull back, lads . . . at the double now, pull back!'

His men needed no urging. No one wanted to be left behind in this desert waste and at the mercy of the Indians and the natives. They all knew what happened to lone Englishmen captured by the locals. A quick death was a blessing.

Now the Indians rallied. They thought they had their surprise attackers on the run. They began to rise from the sand, firing as they did so. McLeod cursed. Urging his men to ever greater efforts, he retreated very slowly, snapping off quick shots to left and right from his big revolver whenever it appeared the Indians were about to attempt to outflank them.

The chatter of the Vickers machine guns grew ever louder. McLeod flung a glance behind him. He could see the tracer cutting the darkness in a lethal morse, but no sign of the attackers. Perhaps they weren't the Indians after all. Perhaps some local tribesmen, eager for revenge and loot, had joined in the fight on the side of the Indians.

But the dour Scot had no time for such considerations now. His primary task was to get his handful of men back to the relative safety of the ancient armoured cars and back to base. Something had gone seriously wrong and he knew that time was of the essence.

An Indian tried to rush him, cursing fluently, teeth an unnatural white in the glowing darkness. McLeod paused and fired from the hip. The Indian seemed to rise from the ground, his rifle tumbled from suddenly nerveless fingers. Still he remained standing, dark face contorted with unbearable pain. McLeod had no time for mercy. He fired again and this time the Indian went down, bowled over backwards, blood spurting from a great hole ripped in his skinny belly. McLeod and his men pushed on. Later McLeod was never very clear how he had managed it with only one of his little band wounded in the arm, but he did, and then they were clambering frantically on their armoured cars, while the two gunners whirled their turrets round, firing burst after burst into the darkness. Five minutes later they were on their way, leaving the sound of firing behind by the second, and McLeod was at last able to put on the headset and listen to Jeeves personally explaining what had happened that night.

'The bloody balloon's gone up at last, McLeod,' Jeeves snorted, voice distorted by static, as if suddenly there were scores of other radios in operation around the great British base. 'That treacherous greasy swine in Baghdad has revolted, probably with outside aid. Anyway, our recce planes report – the bloody only two we've got – report he has seized all official buildings in the capital, including our legation etc. and, more importantly, the Iraqi Army has begun to march on us.'

As the armoured car jolted and bumped its way across the rough track, McLeod realized just how serious the situation was. Jeeves wouldn't have talked to him like this in clear if it hadn't been. For the static in the line indicated that some of the Iraqi advance units, probably their signals, were already in position around Habbaniyah and they'd be obviously picking up Jeeves' transmission.

'We need every man we can get back here. You know our rotten position at base, McLeod. Everybody counts.'

McLeod did. Jeeves probably had half a hundred aircraft. But they were all obsolete and worn out, used for so long in training young pilots to do their bumps and grinds, but they were the only offensive arm Jeeves possessed, providing he could turn them into makeshift bombers and fighters and that his trainee pilots, some with only a couple of dozen flying hours in their logbooks, were capable of flying offensive low-level missions. It would be a tall order. He could see that Jeeves would need every car of the armoured car squadron to give him extra firepower till relief came to Habbaniyah, if it ever did.

'All right.' Jeeves' final words sounded depressed. 'You know the score. They're out there somewhere. Watch your back, McLeod.' There was a sudden crump, which McLeod recognized over the radio as artillery fire, and for a moment he feared that the position from which Jeeves was speaking had been hit. Then the air commodore came back on the air again with, 'They've started shelling us, McLeod . . . Best of luck . . . Over and out . . .'

The radio went dead, leaving a worried McLeod to ponder the new problem that had just arisen. Just like the air commodore, he had been expecting trouble from that rat Raschid Ali el Ghailani for a long time now. With Britain's power waning rapidly in the Middle East ever since the Germans had gone into Africa and beaten the Eighth Army, which led to a rising wave of Arab nationalism, one hadn't needed a crystal ball to guess what might happen. But why had Raschid Ali been in such a hurry when the British *might* still be in a position to send reinforcements from India, as they had done back in the '20s to bolster their forces in Iraq? McLeod knew it was hardly likely that British Far Eastern Command would be able to do so, but he knew his Iraqis. They wouldn't gamble on anything risky unless they possessed all the aces.

As the lead armoured car jolted and bumped ever closer to the base, by peering through the firing slit in vehicle's turret,

McLeod could see the dark smoke of the artillery barrage rising on the dawn horizon where the great base lay. He wondered whether Raschid Ali might be expecting new and unexpected allies to be joining him in his new attempt to rid Iraq of the British. Had these mysterious Indians something to do with the matter? Who had dropped them by parachute into the middle of Iraq's waste lands? Was it the Vichy French in Syria, acting on German orders? Admiral Darlan of the French Navy, the real power in pro-German Vichy France, was a notorious anglophobe. They said it was because his grandfather had been killed by Nelson's fleet at the Battle of Trafalgar in 1805.

McLeod allowed himself a tight grin. The reason seemed absurd, but then the Frogs had long memories for such things, just as his fellow Scots had. Then his grin vanished as he pondered the mystery more. But if the French in Syria hadn't sent these strange Indians, who had? Could it have been the Germans in far away Europe, a couple of thousand miles away? But to what purpose? Even if they were somehow to help Raschid Ali, and his revolt did succeed, what good would that do the Huns all that way away? Iraq under the rebels wouldn't have that much influence on the conduct of the war in the Middle East. Naturally, it might affect oil supplies to the Eighth Army in Egypt, but that would be about it.

In the end a puzzled and worried McLeod gave up. There were too many imponderables, too many questions without answers. He concentrated on looking for the first signs of trouble, for he knew that trouble lay ahead. How much, even that old Iraq hand, Squadron Leader McLeod, could hardly have realized on that hot day in the last week of April 1941.

BOOK TWO

SS Assault Battalion Wotan Marches

One

'Willya take yer eyes off them tits on that Greek gash,' Sergeant Schulze ordered, peering upwards at the Acropolis, 'and get a gander at that place.' He indicated the ruin on the hilltop and added, 'That's culture, Matzi. Now we're getting around to foreign parts, you ought to start to appreciate such things, you Bavarian barnshitter.'

Corporal Matz of SS Assault Battalion Wotan was not impressed. He preferred the melon-like breasts of the dark-eyed Athenians who were ogling their new German conquerors without the slightest inhibition. 'The Tommies must have bombed the shit out of the place,' he answered. 'It's a real bleeding ruin, ain't it?'

Schulze sighed. 'Great crap on the Christmas tree, ain't you frigging ignorant, Matzi! That's not a frigging bomb ruin. That's an ancient temple or something—' He paused abruptly as one of the admiring Greek girls bent suddenly and showed a length of tanned naked thigh. He swallowed hard. 'Holy strawsack!' he hissed. 'Did you see that – legs going right up to her arse.'

The wrinkled little Bavarian corporal grinned and said, 'Now yer talking my language, Schulzi. Culture means nothing to yer normal hairy-arsed stubble-hopper. All he wants is his beer, baccy and beaver – especially beaver.' He grabbed his flies, as if to emphasize his point. 'And when you look at all the free gash around here, Schulze, yer wonder why people waste their time on bits of old stone, when they could be in a nice comfy bed practising yer old two-backed beast.'

Schulze looked thoughtful, all cultural considerations fleeing his mind immediately, as he visualized himself naked, pumping

47

some nubile Athenian lady – also split-assed naked – full of his love juices. 'Yer've said a true word there, Matzi. Sad as it sounds, we've got no time for such cultural matters. When yer common-or-garden stubble-hopper's got a real blue-veiner, a diamond-cutter, a cock that's as sharp as a razor, there's only one thing for it . . .'

'To find some hot gash, Schulzi!' Matz beat the big, red-faced sergeant to it.

'But where? There's a thousand randy Wotan men on the prowl looking for the same thing, Matz,' Schulze objected. 'Why should we be the lucky shits who find it, especially as we've been warned to keep our paws off'n Greek women in case their menfolk take offence and do something nasty to yer sexual equipment?'

'Greek *men*!' Matz sneered. 'Warm brothers running around in skirts like them *evizoni* fellers, or whatever they're called, we fought on the Corinth Canal.'

Schulze sniffed as he remembered Wotan's assault crossing of the Greek canal only a week or so before, and the desperate attempt of Greek soldiers in white skirts with pompoms on their shoes to stop them. It had been a massacre, especially when the 'Vulture', Wotan's CO, had ordered the regiment's flame-throwing tanks into action. As some of Wotan's veterans had called in the crude fashion of the old stubble-hoppers, 'Anybody fancy fried Greek for breakfast, comrades?' No one had. 'Well, we're finished with fighting for the time being, old house. It's up to us to enjoy ourselves now, whatever the rear-echelon stallions –' he meant the staff – 'say. Let's get a skinful and start looking for some of the other. Not much pleasure in life for us poor old broken-down stubble-hoppers, is there?'

'You can say that again, Schulzi,' Matz agreed. 'Let's get on with it.'

But, intent as they were on pleasure this fine April afternoon, the two veterans could not help noticing the activity all around them. Out in Athens bay, the military small craft came and went, bringing in more troops and supplies. Staff cars rolled down the main avenues, filled with self-important staff officers, their briefcases bulging with documents, the red stripe of the Greater German General Staff running down the side of the elegant breeches. As Schulze complained after clicking to attention and saluting yet another monocled senior staff officer, 'Holy shit, where they all coming from? The place's crawling with the rear-echelon bastards in their frigging fancy pants.'

Next to him, Matz relaxed and said somewhat mournfully, 'Don't ask where they come from, Schulzi. Ask why they're here.' He slipped the bottle of ouzo out of his pocket and took a hefty swig at it, his prominent Adam's apple going up and down rapidly like an express lift.

Schulze watched him enviously, licking his suddenly dry lips. 'Greedy, selfish bastard,' he commented without rancour. 'All right, why *are* they here in Athens, birdbrain?'

'Cos the swine are gonna send Wotan into action again. After all, we are the Führer's fire brigade – always sent where the action's hottest.'

'Führer's frigging fire brigade!' Schulze snorted, and made an obscene gesture with his middle finger, which looked like a hairy pork sausage. 'Frig it!' he added impatiently. 'Let 'em do what they like. We're gonna get ourselves tucked up in bed with a couple of Greek whores down here at the harbour. I'm gonna get my head in between a pair of big Greek tits and know no more pain. *Los, Kamerad!*'

Captain Kuno von Dodenburg, head of the First Company, which the two comrades belonged to, was equally puzzled that hot afternoon in Athens. Tall, blond, handsome in that typical arrogant supercilious manner of the regular SS officer, he obeyed the summons to attend the briefing at the Hotel St George, the new German Army HQ in Athens. Fingering his new Knight's Cross, awarded for his bravery in the recent fighting, he was puzzled by the sudden urgent summons to a top-level briefing.

Wotan deserved a rest, he told himself. Their casualties had been high during the long battle right through Yugoslavia and down into Southern Greece, before they had finally flung the Tommies out of the country and the Greek Army had

surrendered. The regiment needed new equipment, reinforcements and time to regain its strength. Naturally von
Dodenburg was as eager as most young SS officers to gain
a reputation and ever new glory. For that reason, he was
proud of having 'cured his throat-ache' and having been
awarded the Knight's Cross by the Führer himself. All the
same, he was concerned about Wotan, and in particular his
own First Company, and the losses they had suffered in the
campaign. Wotan might be the elite of the elite, but he didn't
want his men to suffer unnecessarily by being thrown into
any new action for which he knew they weren't prepared at
this moment.

Blinking a little in the sudden gloom after the bright
Mediterranean sunshine outside, von Dodenburg acknow-
ledged the sentries' salute and passed into the foyer of the
grand hotel, where the rest of Wotan's officers were beginning to assemble, drifting slowly into the conference room.

The CO, Colonel Geier – known behind his back as the
'Vulture', due to his name and great beak of a nose, which
dominated his sensualist's face – was waiting for them,
surveying each new group through his silver monocle, as if
he were trying to see something in their young arrogant faces,
known only to himself.

Von Dodenburg exchanged a few words with one of the
other company commanders, who, like himself, didn't like the
CO. Out of the side of his mouth, the former whispered, 'He's
already gone and got himself a Greek pretty boy. One of the
waiters here, they say.' He shook his head. 'The man's a
disgrace to the SS, Kuno. Fancy having a CO who's a warm
brother.' He meant a homosexual.

Von Dodenburg nodded his understanding. Among the
battalion's officers, it was known that on his leaves the Vulture
haunted Berlin's railway stations looking for those powdered
pretty teenagers with their tight trousers and plucked eyebrows,
who catered to the perverted tastes of his kind. But the Vulture
had been one of the few regular army officers of the
Wehrmacht, with long military training behind him, who had
volunteered for the SS at the beginning of the war, when the

Black Guard had needed such men. Naturally, von Dodenburg knew that the Vulture had only done so to gain more rapid promotion; the beak-nosed, monocled colonel had no feeling for the holy cause of the New Germany. Still, he had led Wotan to victory after victory in Poland, Holland, France and now here in Greece; and that was what counted for the High Command. His perverted tastes had been overlooked and quietly brushed under the carpet.

Von Dodenburg pulled a face, as if he had just smelled something very unpleasant. The boy, obviously the Vulture's new 'lover', had come mincing in, bearing some sort of a message for the CO on a silver tray. He bowed in his too-tight trousers and presented the tray to the Vulture. The latter smirked and von Dodenburg could have sworn it took all the CO's will power to prevent him reaching out and stroking the pretty boy's young cheek.

The Vulture forgot his lover. He clicked to attention and cried in that harsh, high-pitched nasal tone of his, '*Meine Herren, geben Sie acht.*' Immediately the chatter died away; the Vulture was a stickler for discipline in the old-fashioned Prussian fashion. He expected immediate obedience and he got it from young SS officers.

The CO wasted no time. 'You are perhaps surprised that you have been summoned here today. Rightly so. The regiment has fought hard and deserves a rest – you, too.' He grinned at them with his horse teeth; it wasn't a pleasant sight. 'Unfortunately for you, you're not going to get it. The Führer, in his infinite wisdom, has decided SS Assault Battalion Wotan must carry on the fight – *now*.' Again he gave them his horsey grin.

Von Dodenburg could have punched him. The man took every available opportunity to make fun of Germany's saviour, Adolf Hitler. Didn't he realize what the Führer had done for Germany? Didn't he know that Hitler had restored Germany's faith in itself and had made the Fatherland Europe's leading country in a few short years? The man was an absolute cynic. Soon the time must come when the new National Socialist state had to reckon up with perverts like Colonel Geier.

'Why Wotan, you might ask,' the Vulture continued, seemingly completely unaware of the resentment and animosity of his young officers. 'I shall tell you. Because we know our business, better than any other formation in the Greater German *Wehrmacht*. And what is our business?'

Again he answered his own question. 'It is to spearhead an attack, the few of us leading the mass of the German Army.' He smiled cynically at his listeners, who were now tense, eager to find out what new assignment the Vulture, pervert that he was, had dreamed up for them.

But the Vulture was not in a hurry to disclose the details himself. Instead he announced, 'I have someone who will speak to you first. Give you a few details of the importance and full extent of this operation which we will spearhead.' He nodded to the adjutant. The latter went out hurriedly into the former lounge off the conference hall.

Von Dodenburg frowned. It was typical. He always played these games with his officers, holding his cards close to his skinny chest. He presumed that the Vulture's attitude was typical of that of other warm brothers. After all, being a 'Paragraph 175-er'* could mean a long prison sentence in one of the notorious concentration camps where the authorities sent the work-shy, political opponents, habitual criminals and perverted scum, the outcasts of society.

Suddenly the young captain started, his problems with the CO abruptly flung to the winds. The adjutant had returned. At his side there was a smart second lieutenant dressed in a brand-new uniform, as if he had just been commissioned into the *Wehrmacht*. But it wasn't the smart uniform, which contrasted with their battle-worn ones, that caught his attention. It was the officer's headgear – of a kind that he had never seen before in the *Wehrmacht*. The young officer was wearing a turban! Above a face that was decidedly very brown – and that colour obviously didn't come from the hot Greek sunshine.

All around von Dodenburg, there were gasps of surprise

* The German legal paragraph in criminal law relating to homosexuals.

from the young officers, as the Vulture announced, 'Gentlemen, I'd like to introduce you to Second Lieutenant – er – Singh, who will say a few words to you now.' He nodded to the turbaned officer, who now proceeded to surprise the SS men yet again. For when he spoke, he spoke in German in an accent that was educated and almost perfect, save that his intonation was clearly un-German.

'Gentlemen,' he said, smiling at them with his perfect white teeth, 'I am sure you are surprised to see me in German uniform, but I can assure you that there are plenty more of us who are prepared to lay down our lives for the German cause, and that of a free Indian homeland. Three thousand of us, to be precise.' He held up his arm so that they could see the insignia the young officer bore on the upper part of his immaculate tunic.

It was a shield, divided into the three colours of a flag that von Dodenburg couldn't recognize. Surmounted on the flag was a bright springing tiger, above which were the words, *Freies Indien.* 'Free India,' von Dodenburg repeated to himself, wondering what this strange 'Free India' represented, and, in particular, this educated young officer – and what the connection was between him, his organization and the mission which was soon going to be revealed to the officers of SS Assault Regiment Wotan.

The Indian officer dropped his arm and got on with his explanation with almost Prussian efficiency. 'Free India is a brigade-strength formation made up of former soldiers of the British colonial Indian Army. They are all battle-trained and experienced in desert warfare. After they had been taken prisoner by the *Afrikakorps*, all of them immediately volunteered for the German Army, to help Germany free their homeland, groaning under the boot of the English oppressor . . .'

Von Dodenburg caught the look of utter cynicism on the Vulture's ugly face, as he watched the young officer proudly explain that the refugee Indian politician Chandra Bose, who had escaped British imprisonment in his homeland, had had his idea to form a legion of the Indian freedom fighters eagerly accepted by *Reichsführer SS*, their ultimate chief, Heinrich

53

Himmler. It was typical of the Vulture, von Dodenburg told himself. He was concerned solely with his own career – 'Gentlemen, I want to be a general like my father before I die' – and his handsome young boys. The Vulture had nothing but contempt for ideals and great causes.

Then von Dodenburg forgot the Vulture as the young Indian officer announced proudly, face radiating utter confidence in his words, '*Meine Herren*, it is our destiny, the elite of *Reichsführer* Himmler's SS, and the best young men my homeland can provide, together to destroy the colonial might of the cruel British Empire.' He broke off, chest heaving, eyes gleaming, and in the sudden silence, von Dodenburg could hear the shocked gasps of the officers all around him. *The SS and a bunch of inferior black men fighting together? Impossible!*

Two

'Some of my Indian comrades,' Singh continued his excited explanations, 'have already made a reconnaissance of the main bases of the English oppressors in Iraq. There is one at Shaibah near the port of Basra, to which the English could send troops from India in an emergency. The other is at Habbaniyah, where the English maintain their air force. That is the more important of the two. From it, they could send their aircraft to bomb Baghdad, which is some thirty minutes flying time away from the base . . .'

Von Dodenburg listened to the handsome young Indian with a certain amount of disbelief, which was obviously shared by the younger SS officers around him. They were clearly not used to being lectured like this by a man who, despite his obvious education and fluent German, was to them a member of an inferior race – a nigger. Colonel Geier, the Vulture, on the other hand, listened entranced, though von Dodenburg guessed that his interest in Lieutenant Singh was probably more sexual than strategic. Yet none of the bored, arrogant SS officers dared raise any objection. All of them knew it wouldn't be wise to cross the Vulture. He'd make life hell for anyone who did. So, despite their disdain and prejudice, they listened in silence, while Singh warmed to his subject.

'It is then our intention to put most pressure on the Habbaniyah base—'

'*Our*,' someone next to von Dodenburg commented bitterly. 'Did you hear that black bastard say "our"? What cheek!'

'Hold your trap,' von Dodenburg hissed out of the side of his mouth, as the Vulture turned his head to find out who had made the comment, eye glaring angrily behind his monocle.

55

'*However,*' Singh went on, 'the Iraqis are not the bravest of soldiers. It will be the task of SS Assault Battalion Wotan and the men of the Free India Legion to support them and encourage them to attack without incurring losses ourselves.' He frowned, his handsome brown face puzzled. 'I have heard that we are to be used later for more important tasks. Therefore we must keep our losses to a minimum.'

Now it was the Vulture's turn to frown, and von Dodenburg made a hasty guess that there was more to this new assignment than some obscure sideshow in the desert. Not that he had time to consider the matter in any detail. For the Vulture, forcing a smile at the handsome Indian officer, said a little icily, 'Please continue with the main subject, my dear Lieutenant Singh.'

Singh returned the smile, not realizing what dangerous territory he was entering by responding to the Vulture's perverted overtures. '*Jawohl, Obersturmbannführer,*' he snapped, and continued as ordered, still eager to impart his knowledge of the coming operation to his listeners, apparently unable to realize that these supercilious SS officers, the elite of the German Army, were not impressed.

'As I have just said, the Iraqis are not the bravest and most ardent of soldiers. Therefore we must make them fight.' He smiled, displaying those brilliant white teeth of his in what he presumably thought was a winning manner. 'How? But first let me tell you a little tale from my homeland. When my country was ruled by its own masters, cruel as they may have been, they had many ways to make their subjects do as they wished. For instance, there was a form of torture they used which was dreaded by even the bravest of my people.'

Von Dodenburg groaned inwardly. God, had the Indian no sense? He had obviously been educated in Germany. Yet he seemed to be unable to comprehend the German mentality. Germans, especially of the SS, didn't want to be lectured on supposedly quaint Indian customs. He put his hand to his head and wished he was back in the centre of Athens with bustling cafes and pretty girls, ogling one of them in the hope of taking her to bed before the fighting commenced yet again.

'A man would be stripped naked at the Rajah's request, forced to kneel down in chains and then a pot containing a half-starved rat was fixed, hermetically sealed, to his bottom.' Singh smiled at his audience, who, now beginning to stir somewhat uneasily in their seats, were listening intently to the Indian's lecture for the first time. 'When the rat refused to do what it was intended to do, a red-hot poker was thrust through the little hole in the pot. Now, this would make the rat do anything to escape being burned. It would run across the prisoner's naked buttocks, which would tickle at first, until the frenzied rat started biting his bottom to get away from the burning poker.' Singh smiled winningly again, as if he were fully convinced that his audience were thoroughly enjoying his tale from pre-British India. Behind von Dodenburg, someone said thickly, 'Himmler must be mad to give us this crazy man . . . I think I'm going to be sick.'

Von Dodenburg tried to ignore the voice as Singh continued with his terrible account. 'The rat tries and tries to get away by biting and biting. But there was no way out. Then the rat, it was said, would start enjoying the taste of blood, become intoxicated with it, spurred on by the poker trying to burn it, until the frenzied creature finds the only way out.' Singh paused and delivered his punchline. 'The natural exit – the man's backside!'

'Oh my God!' the officer who had complained before groaned. 'Can't anyone stop the black devil?'

But no one could. Singh's awful account held them in its grip, fascinated them, as they listened ashen-faced, almost as if they were hypnotized by it. 'So,' he ended at last, 'both rat and man die at the same time, but only after the human being has suffered, say, half an hour of superlative torture – unless he has succumbed to a haemorrhage or madness before that happens.'

Singh fell silent and gazed at his audience, now wrapped in a shroud of shocked silence, all save von Dodenburg, who was outraged at the Indian's tale of such perverted torture. He kicked back his chair and, braving the Vulture's wrath, as the latter turned to see who had made the noise, demanded in a harsh voice, '*Herr Leutnant*, what has all this – er – nonsense from the past got to do with whatever operation we are soon going to undertake?' Von Dodenburg's lean face twitched suddenly with barely concerned anger. 'Please tell me that, will you?'

Lieutenant Singh was in no way put out by that harsh demand. He smiled – the handsome young Indian seemed to smile a great deal – and said, 'Certainly, I shall tell you, sir. We will have to be that rat, making the Iraqis more frightened of us than they are of the damned English. They will not attack if we don't make them do so. Then we must frighten them into doing so. Thus we do not suffer the casualties they will in order to achieve victory.'

'And how do we make them fear us so greatly?' von Dodenburg commenced, but the Vulture shut him up sharply with, 'That's enough, von Dodenburg! Lieutenant Singh has given a perfectly satisfactory explanation of our intentions in Iraq. After all, whatever way it is to be done, it should be in the interest of every officer in this room that SS Assault Battalion Wotan should suffer as few casualties as possible.' He paused very slightly and then added, almost as if he were speaking to himself, 'Then who knows, gentlemen, when Wotan will need every man it can muster.' He turned again to Singh. 'Thank you, Lieutenant, for an excellent exposé. Perhaps you and I can talk in more detail once this briefing is over?'

'Why, certainly, sir. Yessir, I should be very glad to do so, *Obersturmbannführer*.'

Under his breath, von Dodenburg cursed. He knew the Vulture. For a while at least the handsome young Indian was going to be his bosom friend until the inevitable break came and the Indian would be sacrificed by the CO. For, as sexually predatory as he was, the Vulture was still no fool. When danger loomed up for his career – his aim to become a 'general just like my old father did', as he often boasted in the officers' mess – the Vulture would strike and remove that danger remorselessly.

A few minutes later, they had come to attention, saluted the Vulture with a self-satisfied Lieutenant Singh grinning happily at the CO's side, and left the briefing room, blinking in the glare of the midday sun, each man preoccupied with his own thoughts. For even the thickest of Wotan's officers knew that they were being prepared for a mission: a kind of mission that they had yet to experience in nearly two years of total war.

Von Dodenburg set his cap at the usual rakish angle, favoured by the arrogant, confident young bloods of SS Wotan, though at that moment he felt very uncertain. What kind of assignment had they really been given, he asked himself. For it was clear from Singh's briefing that they were to be involved in some kind of combined operation on what seemed to him the other side of the world. But how were they going to get there? What was to become of their armour? Then it was the dash and the skilled use of their armour which had made SS Wotan feared by the enemy and favoured by the Führer, who had often praised Wotan as the 'elite of the elite' – 'my very own fire brigade' – sent to the front, where the danger was most acute. Von Dodenburg shook his head, even ignoring the shy glances of a very pretty Greek girl, ripe for picking, bursting out, it seemed, of her expensive Paris frock. A lot of questions, he told himself a little miserably, with damned few answers to them.

But Kuno von Dodenburg had not long to dwell on the implications of that briefing. For a well-known voice broke into his reverie, with its usual impact, which meant that its owner was either drunk or in trouble. 'Schulze, the big rogue,' he muttered, even as Schulze came staggering round the corner, drunkenly pushing a wicker-basket pram in front of him, in which reposed Corporal Matz, clutching a bottle of ouzo to his skinny chest like some overgrown, obscene baby, tossing handfuls of worthless Greek coins to the crowds of cheering barefoot kids. But it wasn't the sight of his drunken old hares that gave von Dodenburg pause; he'd seen them drunk time and time again before. It was the two burly military policemen, sweating and angry under their steel helmets, trying to clear the kids out of the way and get at the two SS NCOs.

Von Dodenburg didn't hesitate. Drunk as they were, he'd need the two veterans again in the near future – he was sure of that. '*Still gestanden!*' he ordered. '*Na, wird's bald?*'

The effect of that sharp command penetrated even Schulze's addled brain. The big noncom stumbled to an abrupt stop. Matz, still clutching his precious bottle, fell out of the pram on to the road, where he immediately started to gulp the fiery white alcohol down, a huge grin of absolute delight on his wizened face. 'You Bavarian barnshitter,' Schulze said thickly. 'Can't you see our officer—'

'Trapp, trapp!' Von Dodenburg cut him off sharply as the taller of the two MPs stepped forward, saluted and snapped, 'Drunk and disorderly, sir! Stole one civilian perambulator, attempted to thrust a hand up the mother's dress without permission and—'

'Good . . . good,' Von Dodenburg cut him short a little wearily. How often had he heard similar complaints from other military policemen about the misdeeds of the two old hares. 'Leave them with me. I'll take care of them.'

'Yessir. And the pram, sir?'

'I'll see it's returned.'

The MP hesitated. But not for long. Schulze raised his mighty right haunch, grinned contemptuously at the policeman and then gave one of his celebrated musical farts, well known and respected throughout the SS NCO corps. The policemen fled, as did the kids, leaving Schulze, weakened a little by the effort of that mighty breaking of wind, to gasp, 'Aeroplanes, sir. They're painting frog roundels on the division's Junkers fifty-twos, sir. We're gonna jump out of aeroplanes or something.'

Von Dodenburg nodded his understanding grimly. Now he knew, at least, how they were going to reach their objective, and he didn't like it one bit. On the road, a happy Matz nuzzled his bottle, and then, after a hefty drink, broke into, 'Ain't it a pity she's got only one titty to feed the baby on . . . poor little bugger, he's got only one udder . . .'

Von Dodenburg shook his head, whether in resignation or dismay, he didn't know himself at that particular moment. Then they were off, the elegant young SS officer in the lead, followed by the creaking old pram being pushed drunkenly by Schulze, while, back in his seat, Matz continued to chortle merrily about the 'poor little bugger' with only one udder for nourishment . . .

Three

Now the blood-red ball of the sun had slipped over the horizon and was colouring the sea a thousand feet below a dark, threatening hue. To their front the mountains of the Turkish coast were beginning to flush a dirty pink. Von Dodenburg rubbed the sleep from his eyes and told himself that at least the weather was good as the squadron of Junkers 52s carrying his First Company into the unknown droned on.

They had spent the previous day at Sofia Airport, being prepared for the last stage of their flight to French-held Syria by their new allies the Bulgarians, and it had been obvious that although the Bulgarians were not going to be involved in the Iraq venture, they were preparing for some kind of military operation. There were troops everywhere, and on all sides of the great sprawling airfield, stores were being piled up, while on the perimeter roads, batteries of artillery and tank squadrons rumbled by, coming from the capital heading eastwards. As Schulze had commented to his running mate Matz as they sold Wotan stores to the Bulgarians in exchange for bottles of fiery Bulgarian plum brandy, 'The balloon's soon gonna go up here too, old house. I can smell the lead in the air already.' To which Matz had commented sourly in reply, 'Well, don't smell too much of that frigging plum brandy, *old house*. Cos it's got to last till we get to where we're going – and God frigging well knows where that is, *old house*.'

Now, as the plane rocked with a sudden turbulence caused by thermals rising from the sea below as the air grew warmer, Schulze, too, woke up, licked his parched cracked lips and said to Matz, slumped on the leather-steel seat next to him, 'Pass the flatman.' He meant the flat bottle of plum brandy.

Matz opened his eyes and said, 'What d'yer mean, pass the frigging flatman? You greedy sod, you supped the last of it yersen last night. Without leaving a drop for me.'

Schulze took the complaint calmly. 'Rank hath its privileges,' he answered. 'Remember I'm a sergeant. You're just a lowly corporal, *Corporal* Matz.'

By way of an answer, Matz made a crude suggestion with his dirty middle finger. It was an obscene suggestion that Schulze ignored, remarking only, 'Can't, Corporal Matz. Got a double-decker bus up there already.' He laughed.

Despite his worries, von Dodenburg smiled at the interchange. Matz and Schulze always acted as if they were the worst of enemies, but when the chips were down and the shit started to fly, they were prepared to fight to the death for one another. They were true comrades. Then he dismissed the two rogues and concentrated on his problems.

His knowledge of the overall plan was limited. They would fly to Damascus in Syria, refuel once more there, and then, avoiding British air patrols if there were any, they'd slip across the border with French pilots at the controls of the Junkers – the French knew more of the Iraq border area than their own *Luftwaffe* pilots. Once safely over the frontier, they'd land in the desert. Here Lieutenant Singh, still asleep at the moment, would guide them to where his own 'Free Indians' were camped. Together the Wotan troopers and the Indians would exert pressure on the rebel Iraqis to attack and capture the British airbase at Habbaniyah. What Wotan was supposed to do after that, von Dodenburg had only the vaguest of ideas. But he felt sure the Führer wouldn't want to waste one of his elite SS battalions on such a godforsaken place as Iraq. There had to be more to the coming campaign than that.

He looked to where the handsome Indian still slept and told himself that the young officer knew more than he did. He'd seen him deep in conversation with the Vulture more than once in the last forty-eight hours before they had set off: conversations which had ended abruptly whenever anyone came close to the two officers. And it was certain that it was not just sexual overtures that the Vulture was making to Singh. There was more to it than that.

For a while as the plane droned on, von Dodenburg let his mind wander. He wondered how the new recruits, the youngsters who had joined his First Company to replace the losses of the Balkan campaign, would fare in combat. He considered how his veterans would take to the strict water rationing they would have to impose in the desert; how they'd fare against the British without armour or heavy weapons. Slowly his eyes started to close once more as he was lulled into the doze occasioned by the steady boring progress of the old three-engined transport eastwards. To his right, Sergeant Schulze began to snore once more. Not for long.

Suddenly, startlingly, there was the abrupt clatter of machine-gun fire. Von Dodenburg woke from his new doze with a start. He was just in time to catch a glimpse of a single-engined fighter flashing back the port, trailing white smoke behind it, as the fuselage flooded with the acrid stink of burnt cordite and cold air. On the floor a young reinforcement writhed in his death throes, choking on his own bright red blood, his plea '*Mama . . . Mama*,' barely audible as he died in front of them.

In an instant all was confusion as the young *Luftwaffe* pilot broke formation, Next moment he was diving to the bright blue sea below, as yet another fighter came bursting through the Junkers' formation, machine guns spitting angry blue fire at the cumbersome transports. But they, too, were reacting, scattering crazily, their gunners answering the enemy fire the best they could. For they knew they were hopelessly outgunned by their attackers, and at least a couple of hundred kilometres per hour slower.

At the controls of von Dodenburg's Junkers, the pilot fought desperately to shake off his attacker and at the same time bring the three-engined plane out of her dive before she smacked straight into the sea, which was looming larger and larger by the instant.

On his seat, holding on to a spar for all he was worth, von Dodenburg willed him to succeed as the pilot heaved and heaved at the joystick, almost standing up in his seat, his shoulder muscles threatening to burst through the thin material of his coverall at any moment.

Again there was the clatter of machine-gun fire, and slugs ripped the length of the Junkers' fuselage. Abruptly, ragged silver holes appeared as if by magic and men fell writhing to the deck, as their attacker zoomed away in a tight turn, perhaps believing he had finished the Junkers off for good. But he hadn't.

Slowly, awesomely slowly, the plane began to come out of that dive of death. Its every rivet and panel howled in protest at the tremendous strain. White-faced with fear, eyes bulging out of their heads like men demented, the troopers clung to their seats, some howling without restraint, a few even praying.

Suddenly the pilot slumped into his seat. For a moment von Dodenburg thought it was just with relief at the fact he had pulled the plane out of that fatal dive. Then he saw he was wrong. There was deep-red blood pumping from the *Luftwaffe* man's right shoulder. He had been hit – badly. '*Scheisse!*' he cursed. None of them could fly a plane. If the pilot went now, their goose would be cooked. 'Lieutenant Singh,' he called urgently, as the British fighter came in yet again, determined to knock the German plane out of the sky. 'Attend to the pilot.'

'Sir.' Singh didn't hesitate. He sprang from his seat and rushed to aid the wounded man.

Von Dodenburg craned his neck and cursed as the enemy fighter opened up yet again, angry purple flame rippling the length of its wings, as its eight Browning machine guns burst into frenetic life.

Tracer slammed into the port wing. The engine spluttered. For a moment von Dodenburg's heart stopped. Then the damaged engine came to life once more, but now he could see the black smoke pouring from it in thick clouds. He knew it wouldn't last much longer. Von Dodenburg said a quick prayer that the wounded pilot, with Singh's aid, could keep the crippled Junkers in the air till they were over land. He'd feel safer if the pilot could ditch the plane on terra firma. But that wasn't to be.

Suddenly the port engine cut out for good. For one long, frightening moment, as the plane lurched sharply to starboard, von Dodenburg thought the wounded pilot wouldn't be able to hold the Junkers. But with Singh's help he did. Now, with black smoke trailing behind her, the Junkers headed for the land. Still the British fighter plane didn't let up. Jockeying for position, it clung to the dying plane's tail, trying to get in that killing burst that would tear the Junkers out of the sky.

Somehow or other the pilot managed to toss the plane from side to side every time the fighter was about to fire that final murderous volley. How the pilot did it, dying as he was at the controls, von Dodenburg never found out. Besides, he had no time to consider the matter now. Shouting above the whine of the dying plane and the chatter of the fighter's eight machine guns, he ordered, 'Prepare to ditch . . . For God's sake, *prepare to ditch!*'

The survivors of the First Company needed no urging. The ground was racing up to meet them at a frightening rate now. They raised their feet and buried their faces in their clasped arms, tensed for the inevitable impact. Von Dodenburg made one last check, as behind them the British fighter plane gave up and broke to the right, its pilot obviously satisfied that the Junkers and everyone on board her was doomed. Then he too took up the ditching position, his heart pounding in the knowledge that the next few minutes decided whether he would live or die. Now he had lost all control over his young life. He was at the mercy of fate. He could only crouch tensed here and wait for the inevitable to happen. He gave a hollow laugh. What was it they always proclaimed in SS Assault Battalion – *march or croak*? Now he was no longer able to do that.

The roar of the surviving two motors ceased abruptly. It was replaced by the eerie sound of wind whistling through the bullet holes in the Junkers' fabric.

With that air, von Dodenburg, head bent into his arms, could smell the scent of the land, the mixture of herbs and exotic plants. For a moment the scene took his mind off what was to come. Abruptly Singh's cry alerted him. He tensed, as Singh repeated in a fragile broken voice, 'This is it. We—' The rest of his words were cut off by a tremendous bang as the Junkers hit the earth. Its undercarriage took the impact and the three-engined plane bounced upwards once more like an express lift. A moment later it hit the ground once more. This time the undercarriage snapped and collapsed immediately. The fuselage slammed to the ground and then they were racing forward at a hundred kilometres an hour, as the dying pilot tried frantically to keep control of the plane. To no avail. It slithered and shimmied forward, the rocks and the rough terrain tearing the guts out of it.

Men screamed. Others were thrown out of their seats and slammed against the walls, to lie there in grotesque positions like broken dolls. Desperately, von Dodenburg hung on. To his front, Schulze roared, 'Fuck this for a game o' soldiers . . . I'm getting off.' He wasn't. Next moment he slammed his shaven head against the shattered fuselage and went out like a light.

Then it happened. The Junkers hit the side of a rock wall. Its crazy progress across that wild barren landscape, trailing bits and pieces of severed metal behind it, ended. With a great lurch and rending of torn metal, the rump rose high into the air. Something struck von Dodenburg hard across the face. He yelled with acute pain. Next moment everything went black.

Four

Groggily von Dodenburg pulled his way out of the smoking wreckage of the fuselage. There were dead and dying men everywhere, sprawled out in the wrecked plane, some of their faces bloody unrecognizable masks, as if someone had thrown a handful of strawberry jam at them.

For a few moments, von Dodenburg wanted to do nothing but get out and breathe in the clear air to escape the cloying petrol fumes of that place of death. His mind wouldn't function any further than that. A big hand like a small steam shovel grabbed his and led him out, as if he were a very old and feeble person. Under other circumstances, he would have shaken it off angrily. Not now. He felt the need for any support that could be given to him. Gratefully he let himself be led to a stunted olive tree where his benefactor – it was Schulze, his broad face a mess of blood – stood him against it and ordered, 'Breathe in nice and slow, sir. It'll do yer good. Though a good stiff shot of Westphalian *Korn*'d do yer more good.' Schulze gave a great sigh, like a man sorely tried by the injustices of this world.

'Thank you, Schulze,' von Dodenburg heard himself say, as if from a long way off. 'Look after the men . . .' His words dribbled away. Schulze had already gone back to the wreckage and was pulling a heavy panel of metal from a man trapped beneath it.

Von Dodenburg sucked in the clear air gratefully. The black mist which had threatened to overcome him was beginning to dissipate at last, and he knew it was time that he took charge. He had to make some sort of order from this confused mess before any further trouble made its appearance, and he was sure, for what reason he couldn't fathom at that moment, that it would.

About an hour later, von Dodenburg knew the worst. He had lost ten men, with a further five pretty badly hurt – sufficiently so that they couldn't march. The thought of what he would have to do to those poor devils filled him with dread. But for the time being he concentrated on burying the dead, patching up the lightly wounded, and sorting out whatever supplies they might be able to take with them, though what their objective might be, von Dodenburg hadn't the faintest idea. For the moment it seemed to him that they were in the middle of nowhere with sand and scrub stretching as far as the eye could see, without a dwelling of any kind in sight. In the end, he had given Singh, who had recovered from the ordeal of the crash as quickly as the Wotan old hares, the task of trying to establish their position.

Meanwhile, Schulze and Matz were trawling through the wreckage, in theory looking for anything that might be of use for the march. In fact, however, the two old hares were searching for something stronger than the water they had just drained from a shattered radiator and that taken from the water bottles of the troopers killed in the crash. It had been carefully tested before being distributed among the survivors, but so far the two veterans had found only one flask filled with cold tea instead of stale drinking water. As Schulze commented, wiping the beads of sweat from his forehead, 'There ain't no justice for us common-or-garden stubble-hoppers, Matzi. Cold Tommy piss –' he meant tea – 'what good's that to hairy-chested soldiers, I ask yer, comrade.'

Matz shrugged, as if the question was too overwhelming for him to comprehend. Instead he broke into the tuneless monotony of the old ditty, which recounted the tale of the unfortunate young lady called Starkie, '*Who had an affair with a darkie. The result of her sins . . . was a eightsome of twins. Two black and two white and four khaki.*'

Sitting under the shade of the wrecked starboard wing, Lieutenant Singh looked up from the charred bit of map he had found in the dead pilot's cockpit. At that moment, von

Dodenburg happened to glance in that direction. For a few moments he wondered what was going through the Indian's mind after hearing that little ditty, full of racial prejudice. For Singh's face revealed nothing, neither resentment nor hate. But then, von Dodenburg told himself, in the few days since he had first met the Indian lieutenant, Singh had shown nothing of his inner feelings. Admittedly he smiled a lot, as if he might be nervous, though at the same time he took himself and the cause of Free India very seriously. So what did go on in Singh's mind?

Five minutes later Singh called over and told von Dodenburg that he calculated they were somewhere on the border between Syria, Palestine and Iraq. 'From what I have heard from our own people,' he lectured an attentive von Dodenburg, 'it is not the friendliest of places.'

'What do you mean, Lieutenant?' von Dodenburg queried, his mind really concentrating on the awful thing he would have to do soon.

'Like most border people, those pay little loyalty to their official masters. They play off Arabs, Jews, Iraqis –' he shrugged – 'you name it, against one another. Religion means little to them, too. But this does.' He made the continental gesture of counting money with his thumb and forefinger. 'Money, especially gold and silver coins, with which they adorn their womenfolk, that's the religion of those border people, so I have been told.'

Von Dodenburg nodded his understanding. 'Well, work out the route of march for us, Lieutenant. The heat of the day's over. We'd better get moving.'

He didn't wait to see Singh's reaction. Indeed, he had already forgotten what he had just said to the Indian. Now his mind was racing electrically, full of what he had to do next before they left the wreck.

Slowly, his handsome face set and intent, he walked over to where the men who were dying were being sheltered under some stunted olive and camel scrub, cloths over their faces, soaked in precious water, to keep the flies and heat off. One or two of them were still moaning. Fortunately, however, they were unconscious, something for which von Dodenburg was grateful. Slowly the young officer loosened the catch of his pistol holster. Watching him, Schulze, his search for firewater abandoned, felt for his company commander. Twice he had seen officers carry out this horrible task in the campaign through the Balkans, where it had been feared they would have to abandon Wotan's wounded to the Serbs who kept cutting them off in the mountains during the attack on Belgrade. For Wotan, just like the rest of the feared elite SS formations, never left its wounded behind. If they couldn't take the wounded with them, then there was only one other alternative.

Now von Dodenburg was having to face up to that terrible other alternative. Schulze wished he could have done the job for his admired company commander, but he knew that wasn't possible. It was a grim task, to be carried out by an officer only. For a few moments, an officer would play the role of God: decide between life and death for a fellow human being. It was something that the military establishment of the Waffen SS had decreed could only be left to a gentleman and a commissioned officer.

Slowly the young CO approached the first of the dying men, silent beneath the bloodstained tarpaulin which covered him. Gently von Dodenburg bent and removed the covering from his face. The boy, for he was one of the teenage reinforcements, didn't move. Fortunately he was too far gone. It was something for which von Dodenburg was profoundly grateful. He looked down for a moment at the boy he was now going to kill, and then he clicked off his safety. It seemed to make a hell of a row. Still the boy didn't stir. Carefully von Dodenburg bent and placed the muzzle of his pistol at the base of the dying kid's skull. He hesitated only a single moment. His jaw tightened. Next instant he jerked back the trigger of his pistol. The dying man started up as the bullet struck the back of his head. For an instant. He yelled. Not for long. Suddenly, the back of his head disappeared in a welter of dark red blood, through which the shattered bone gleamed like polished ivory.

Von Dodenburg swallowed hard. He felt himself beginning to tremble. The pistol wavered in his blood-splattered hand. Hot green bile welled up in his throat. He told himself he was about to be sick. With an effort of sheer will power, he repressed the feeling.

He killed the next man, trying to make the killing worthy but unable to do so, just wanting to get what amounted to cold-blooded murder over and done with as soon as possible. For in a moment he knew that he'd break under the strain of killing his own soldiers and be unable to carry on.

But the horror had just started. Just as he was about to pull the blanket from number three, the dying man did so himself and he saw that well-known face. It was that of Lance Corporal Heinz, an old hare who had been serving with the Battalion since before the war when von Dodenburg had joined as a callow young second lieutenant straight from the Cadet Academy at Bad Tolz.

Heinz blinked weakly and looked up at von Dodenburg's strained face, seeing the smoking pistol in his right hand. 'Got to be done, sir,' he breathed, the end of his nose a sickly white, a sure indication that he was close to death. 'I don't want to be left to no heathens.' He gasped for breath and closed his eyes for a moment.

Von Dodenburg swallowed hard. The permanent lance corporal – for that was what Heinz had been, always willing to obey orders and move out when the shit was flying in Poland, France, the Balkans and Greece – deserved a better fate than this: to be shot in cold blood by one of his own officers, out in this barren wilderness the very name of which they didn't know. God, it was damned awful.

Heinz's eyes blinked open again. 'Better get on with it, sir,' he said. 'You and the lads'll want to be off before it gets proper dark.'

Von Dodenburg seemed unable to move. At that moment, if he had been able to, he would have dropped the pistol and fled. He hadn't the strength any more to put this old soldier, who had served his battalion so loyally all these years without reward, out of his misery. But Heinz made it easy for him.

'I'll turn, sir,' he breathed, and with a grunt of pain, he turned his dying body so that he lay face downwards, the back of his skull exposed for von Dodenburg to fire that coup de grace.

As if watching someone else going through these last terrible motions, von Dodenburg saw the hand grasping the pistol move towards the vital spot just below the left ear. He watched as the trigger finger turned white as the first pressure was applied to the trigger of the pistol; the slightest hesitancy and then the finger pulling back the trigger the whole way. A thunderous crash, or so it seemed. The back of Heinz's skull bulged. Next moment it exploded in the ruddy welter of blood and gore. Heinz gave a strange sad little sigh and then he was dead.

Five minutes later the survivors, strung out in single file, were on their way into the unknown, led by Lieutenant Singh with his fragment of map: puny little creature set against the infinity of that featureless desert. No one looked back.

BOOK THREE

The Defence

One

The Habbaniyah RAF Base had been under siege for over four days now. The Iraqis had advanced down the main road from the capital as far as the heights to the east of the base, where they had dug their artillery in. But instead of the expected infantry attack, which the RAF staff knew would probably overrun Habbaniyah, because the base simply had not enough infantry or local levies to defend itself against such an assault, all that the Iraqis had done was to pound the RAF positions at regular intervals. It seemed they were working to some timetable – the kind the older RAF men remembered from the Great War, when such artillery shoots had been followed by an infantry attack. That attack had, however, not come.

Air Commodore Jeeves had used the lull to his own best advantage. Swiftly, with his aircraftsmen and some of the trainee pilots working all out, he had transformed his obsolete battered training aircraft into rough-and-ready attack aircraft. Lewis guns had been mounted and bomb racks welded on the trainers. With the handful of instructors acting as pilots, and the trainee pilots as air crew, Jeeves had already launched several sorties against the Iraqi gun positions and their supply convoys bringing men, ammunition and water from Baghdad. The latter bombing attacks had been particularly successful, for the Iraqi army seemed to have no idea of convoy distances or the use of light machine guns as anti-aircraft defence. Twice the primitive bombers and fighter bombers had wiped out enemy convoys, leaving the main road from Baghdad littered with their shattered burning vehicles and the bodies of their soldiers.

Still, as Jeeves told McLeod, back from yet another recce

into the desert behind the Iraqi positions, 'The buggers are not going to sit there for ever, you know, with their thumbs up their arses. They're going to attack in the not so distant future.'

McLeod stopped sucking his old pipe and nodded his grey head in agreement. 'You're right, Air Commodore. Intelligence signalled half an hour ago that the enemy's going to get reinforcements – first-class troops.' He hesitated for a fraction of a second, taking in the 'shit wallahs' truck', an old three-tonner lurching across the field, the great metal drums containing ordure from the other ranks' latrines, bumping up and down in the back. 'German to boot.'

'*German!*'

'That's it, sir. Huns flying in from Greece, via Bulgaria and French Syria. The RAF boys in the Middle East have already reported shooting down one of their transports over the Med.'

Jeeves went brick-red with rage. 'Those bloody Frogs. You can't trust the sods! Fighting the Hun last year, now helping him this one. What can you do with an ally like that?'

'*Former* ally,' McLeod corrected the irate commodore. But the latter wasn't listening.

'What else do we know about these bloody Huns?' he demanded.

'Not much, sir. The info we have so far is that they're sending an SS battalion, perhaps some eight hundred men strong, with the Syrian French helping them over the border into Iraq from the airfield at Damascus. I don't know—' McLeod stopped abruptly and stared at the 'shit wallahs' truck'.

'What is it, McLeod?'

For a moment or two the old Scot didn't reply. His gaze was fixed on the truck.

'Well?' Jeeves demanded.

'It's the shite wallahs. They're driving that lorry as if they'd had a few. The shite from the barrels is flying everywhere.' McLeod gave Jeeves a hefty shove and cried at the top of his voice in sudden alarm. 'Get down everyone! Watch those shit wallahs!' In that same instant he pulled out his service revolver and, standing as if he were back on some peacetime range, pointed the .38 at the man in the back of the truck, dressed in black with a scarf wound across the bottom of his face. But it wasn't the scarf that caught the Scot's attention. It was the tommy gun the man was carrying, which he was now aiming at a group of young officers just emerging from the mess. 'Get to the bluidy ground, will ye!' he cried angrily, and fired in that same instant.

He was too late. The man beat him to the draw. He pressed the trigger of his tommy gun. It burst into frenetic life. Suddenly the air was full of the stink of burned cordite. The officers went down like ninepins, thrashing and cursing in their death agonies.

McLeod fired. The truck's rear tyre exploded as the bullet struck it. The truck careened wildly to the left. McLeod fired again. Its windscreen shattered into a gleaming spider's web of broken glass. Frantically the Iraqi driver fought to keep control. To no avail. With the tommy-gunner hanging on for all he was worth, the truck slammed into the back of a Tiger Moth, attached by a tube to a petrol bowser. *Whoosh.* In a flash, the petrol exploded, wreathing both the truck and the plane in searing blue flame.

The gunman dropped over the side, his body already being consumed by the greedy flames. McLeod didn't give him a chance to escape. 'Bastard,' he snarled, and fired again. The murderer flung up his skinny brown hands as if praying to Allah. But Allah was looking the other way this terrible day. Next instant he slammed to the tarmac, the flames from the burning plane engulfing him in a flash. One second more and the petrol bowser exploded with a thunderous roar. Ordure mixed up with chunks of human flesh splattered everywhere, and then it was over and a brooding silence descended once more on the huge RAF base, as the two officers left the mess for others to clear up, and walked away, both deep in thought.

After a while, McLeod took his old smelly pipe from his mouth and said thoughtfully, 'Commodore, I'd like to make a suggestion.'

'What? Oh, yes,' Jeeves responded. 'Then suggest away.'

'It's obvious, sir, that apart from these pin-prick suicide

attacks, the Iraqis are not going to attack in force until the Huns appear on the scene, if that is what the Jerries intend – and I think they do.'

'Go on, McLeod.'

'Well, sir, if we could locate the Huns before they contact the Iraqis, and can isolate them before they get into the mountain positions, then we'd have a damn good chance of clobbering them with your trainee pilots. They might not be the kind of top-class pilots we're used to, but out in the open desert, even they could bomb the shit out of the Huns, if you'll forgive my French.'

'I will,' Jeeves said with unusual enthusiasm for him. 'That's an excellent idea. We know the Hun from the old war. Once he's dug in, it's one devil of a job to winkle him out.' He frowned. 'But how are you going to locate these Jerries of yours? Iraq's a damned big country.'

'I've thought about that too, sir. The Germans can't go wandering around the desert blindly. They are going to need to contact the Iraqis pretty damned sharpish once they're on the ground, and for that they'll use their radios. What I would need, therefore, sir, would be one of your best RAF wireless operators, able to use a radio-location device.'

'We've not got one,' Jeeves interjected bluntly.

'I know. I've already enquired, sir.'

'Have you just!'

'But I'm sure we've got the skills in the base's WT section to mock up a radio detection van to accompany my armoured cars.'

Jeeves' hard face lit up. 'Of course we have. We can use one of those little utility vans. They're tough little buggers. They don't use much fuel and there'd be enough room in the back to accommodate the radio-detection equipment, I'm sure. McLeod, regard it as done. Now, what's the drill going to be . . . ?'

At five that afternoon, with the sun slowly sinking in the west and great black shadows sweeping across the desert scrub like silent predatory hawks, the patrol was ready to move out. For the last hour, McLeod had checked through their equipment methodically, while Hawkins, the radio operator, had been trying his detector equipment inside the burning interior of the utility van.

Old desert hand that he was, McLeod always did the checking for a long-distance patrol personally. A mistake in the number of jerricans of water, or even the salt tablets which the RAF crews had to take daily, could well spell disaster in the burning heat of the Iraqi desert at midday. He had seen men go mad with heatstroke all too often in his years in the Middle East to risk anything like that happening just on account of a simple oversight.

Over in the mountains, the Iraqi batteries were beginning to fire once again, and it seemed to McLeod as he reached their supplies of Eno's Fruit Salts, which the patrols used to make their stale drinking water more palatable, that the Iraqis were laying on the pressure at last. They were firing more rounds and more accurately. Did that signify anything? Were the plotters in Baghdad, who had started this new rising against the British, putting on the pressure? Or had the Germans arrived? McLeod didn't know. What he did know was that if the pressure was on, he'd have to find those damned Huns that the treacherous Frogs were helping to reach Iraq, sooner rather than later.

At five thirty he finished his check and, as a special treat, produced a bottle of ice-cold light ale for every man of the patrol. The fact that they were setting off on a dangerous patrol into the unknown didn't stop the look of delight in the men's eyes when they saw the beer bottle dripping with condensation. 'Cor, ferk a duck!' 'Red' Brown exclaimed, 'Ice-cold beer. Why, a bloke out here would give his left ball for a bottle of this, Squadron Leader.'

McLeod returned his delighted smile with a somewhat wintry one of his own. 'I'm not asking you to pay that kind of price, Brown. But you deserve it. All of you do. Better enjoy it slowly, lads. You won't be seeing the like for a long time to come.' McLeod didn't realize just how true his words were. Some of them would never savour a bottle of ice-cold beer ever again.

Fifteen minutes later, with the sun a blood-red ball on the horizon, they set off.

By eight that night they had covered ten miles off the road. McLeod thought that they had made good time, and decided it was time for them to bivouac for the night. He wanted the little radio operator to search the airwaves for any signal that the Germans might send, for so far he was searching the area merely by experience and intuition. On the morrow they'd face the shifting sands of the interior and progress would be slow and back-breaking, he knew that of old. Accordingly he didn't want to waste time in the damned shifting sands if he could help it. The constant stop-start of driving through that kind of terrain took the heart out of the stoutest of men.

Glad to stop, the men settled down over their little petrol cookers, making the inevitable 'char', frying tinned Canadian bacon and treating themselves (unknown to them, courtesy of the RAF's officers' mess) to the sweet delight of tinned peaches, while McLeod queried the little radio operator, who now, instead of sweating in the searing heat of the day, was shivering with cold. For now an icy wind was beginning to blow across the desert, and some of the men were already huddled in their sleeping bags, holding the precious warmth of their 'char' in both hands.

'Well?' McLeod demanded. 'Anything, Sparks?'

The little operator, his lips blue with cold, shook his head. 'Not much, sir. Though one thing – there's a lot more traffic than there was when we set out. The airways are fair buzzing with traffic – a lot of it coming from the direction of Baghdad.'

McLeod nodded his approval. 'Anything you could decipher?'

'No sir. But there's this. The hands are different.'

'What do you mean, Sparks?'

'Well, sir, we trained most of the wog operators and we can recognize their "hand" – the way they send morse. They do it on the British Army pattern. But these hands aren't using the British style.' He shivered violently and McLeod took pity on the little man in his thin desert uniform. 'All right, Sparks, go and get yourself some char and a wad. It'll warm you up.'

*　*　*

That night, despite his weariness, the old Scot couldn't sleep. While the rest slept, save for the sentry, who moved around in an attempt to keep warm, he lay with his hands propped beneath his head, staring at the night sky. It was a beautiful night, the sky hard and silver, bright with the light of myriad stars. It was good to lie thus in the warmth of the sleeping bag, protected from the cold outside. It was the kind of feeling he had experienced as a child in the freezing cold manse of his father, warmed by the stone water bottle his mother had slipped under the blankets when his father, the dominie, hadn't been looking; or that he experienced with his wife, poor dead Jenny, killed in the first great London blitz of late 1940, at the same time as his son Jamie had gone missing with the Scottish 51st Highland Division back in France: a whole family wiped out in a matter of six months.

McLeod sucked his false teeth and wished he could have a smoke of his pipe. But he knew that was impossible; it might give their position away to anyone who might be on the lookout for their camp. He told himself he really didn't have much to live for, had he. All he was was a lonely old broken-down middle-aged squadron leader who would never get any further promotion. After all, he was a non-flyer, and promotion always went to pilots. He smiled ruefully. There was nothing he could do about things, but soldier on. As they had said in the trenches in the old war, when he had been a boy, with that fatalism of the frontline soldier who knew he had a mere six weeks to live, 'Roll on death, let's have a crack at the angels.' His smile broadened even more at the memory, and then he turned over and went straight to sleep, at peace at last.

Two

When McLeod awoke that dawn, the weather had changed dramatically. Instead of the bone-chilling cold of the night, with the kind of visibility that made you believe you could see to the end of the world, the dawn was muggy and the desert was covered by a thick yellow haze that reminded the Scot of the sea frets of his Scottish youth. He frowned. It was not the kind of weather that he had expected. Nor was it something that he welcomed.

In fog, his armoured cars were particularly vulnerable to marauding Iraqis. With visibility down to a few yards, they could easily approach an unwary armoured car crew and put them out of action with a grenade thrown into the open turret, or a volley fired at close range into a vehicle's tyres, and by immobilizing it make the stalled armoured car easy meat for the attackers.

Still McLeod knew he had to carry on with his vital mission. The Huns had to be found before they could link up with the Iraqi army besieging the base. With a bit of luck, Jeeves' makeshift aerial strike force might be able to scupper them before that. All the same, he warned his crews, busy shaving and swallowing a hearty breakfast of the usual Canadian tinned bacon, beans and, of course, a mug of their celebrated 'sarnt-major's char': a thick rich brew, made even richer by the addition of a precious tin of Carnation milk.

'Keep the hatches battened down at all times till the fog lifts. I know it's going to be hot in the tin cans,' he lectured his men, 'but it's better being hot than dead. And above all, keep your eyes peeled at all times. If you see any wandering Iraqis, don't bother to challenge, fire at the buggers straight-

away before they can get close to your vehicle. If you don't –'
he attempted a smile, though he had never felt less like smiling
– 'they might well give you a nasty kick in the arse. All right,'
he concluded, 'five more minutes and we're on our way –
and those of you who want to take a shovel for a walk –' he
meant those who had to evacuate their bowels, covering up
the faeces with a shovel – 'don't go out of sight of the vehicles. Okay, get to it.'

McLeod's words had their effect. Now the armoured car
crews went about their duties with understandable nervous-
ness, occasionally glancing over their shoulders when they
'took their shovels for a walk', as if they half expected they
were being followed by a bunch of murderous Iraqi cutthroats.

An hour later, crawling along at a snail-like ten miles an
hour, they were still fighting the yellow fog, and there was
no sign of the usual burning sun, which would have dispersed
it in a matter of minutes. Now everyone was on edge, the
drivers and gunners peering through their slits for the first
sign of the enemy, ready for action at a moment's notice.
McLeod, the old Iraqi hand, shared their nervous apprehension. For he knew just how vulnerable they were crawling
along at this slow pace, shrouded in fog, which could cut them
off from one another in a matter of moments, as it drifted
across the desert. At the same time, however, he was on the
lookout for the first sign of these ellusive Huns who were
supposed to be out in the desert somewhere or other and trying
to make the link-up with the Iraqi forces besieging the base.

Another hour passed with leaden feet. Still the fog had not
lifted. Indeed, a worried McLeod felt it had even thickened,
as they now entered a series of low hills where the fog lingered
in the hollows, coating the sides of their obsolete vehicles
with damp condensation, as if they were in the Highlands of
his native country on some grey November day. Now, because
of the terrain and the fog, they were forced into passing through
the little passes in single file, the drivers of the vehicles barely
able to see the outline of the armoured car in front.

McLeod felt his sense of unease growing. This was ideal
ambush country. A bold attack by a handful of determined

men might well be able to halt the whole strung-out convoy with disastrous results. He started to study the country about and ahead with ever more intense concentration, feeling the damp beads of sweat trickle down the small of his back unpleasantly. More than once he broke the command vehicle's radio silence with, 'Now don't forget, you men, keep those turrets closed, and you gunners, watch both flanks. Clear?'

But the men needed no urging. All of them knew only too well what Iraqis did to British troops taken prisoner. They died – but slowly and very painfully. As they often warned newcomers to the armoured-car section, who hadn't 'got their knees brown' yet, 'Save the last bullet for yersen, mate. It's better to die clean like that than have the wogs working yer over with their frigging knives. Frigging soprano, after they've finished with yer waterworks.' And they would give a dramatic shudder to illustrate their point.

Time dragged. The series of passes through the fog-bound hills seemed endless. McLeod, not an imaginative man usually, felt his nerves begin to tick nervously. Somehow, he couldn't explain exactly why, he started to see shadows reflected through the fog, wavering from one extreme to the other, becoming large and menacing and then diminishing into almost nothing. Above the whine of the car's Rolls Royce engine, he imagined he heard other noises. What they were, he couldn't define. All he knew was that they were frightening, intended him no good. For a few moments he longed to order his driver to go faster, put his foot down and hasten their departure from the passes. But he knew that would upset the others following him, perhaps even cut him off from the other cars. He contained himself and let the driver continue at his snail-like pace.

Then it happened. They had just turned a bend in the pass, with the vehicle in front already round the next curve and the one behind not yet in sight, when his driver cursed – 'Bloody hell!' – and hit the brakes hard. McLeod, startled, nerves jangling, caught a glimpse of a slither of rocks to their front coming down in a mini-avalanche. Next moment the armoured car shuddered to a stop and he heard the sound of boots landing on the steel deck. 'Stand fast,' he gasped, as almost immediately someone began trying to prise the turret hatch open. Other boots ran to the front of the stalled armoured car, while the startled driver frantically tried to start it once again, as someone was attempting to get to the muzzle of their two-pounder cannon.

Shocked as he was, McLeod reacted correctly. 'Gunner,' he yelled over the intercom. 'Swing the turret round. Don't let him get at the muzzle . . . Car Three,' he called to the other car following him round the bend. 'Watch yer step. Open fire at anyone on the deck of my vehicle. *Fire!*'

For a few minutes, everything became a crazy chaos. Desperately their unseen assailants tried to break into the armoured car, while the driver, eyes popping with fear, cursed mightily as he attempted to start up once more, and the first burst of tracer from the follow-up car pattered along the rear of the armoured car like heavy tropical rain on a tin roof. A scream of mortal agony. A heavy thud as one of their attackers slammed to the ground. But suddenly the machine gun stuttered to a stop. McLeod cursed. He knew instinctively what had happened. The gun had jammed. Their ancient equipment, bought years before by a parsimonious British government, had failed them yet again.

The sudden respite encouraged their unseen attackers. Now he could hear their yells and cries as they emerged again from their hiding places in the rocks and assaulted the trapped vehicle once more. This time, however, they tried a new tack. Liquid sloshed against the sides of the stalled armoured car. Suddenly the interior was filled with a cloying smell. 'Jesus wept!' the gunner cried. 'Petrol!'

McLeod's heart sank. He knew instinctively what they were in for. Next moment it happened. A bottle shattered against the side of the armoured car. It would be a home-made Molotov cocktail, being used as igniter. An instant later, it burst into flames with a great whoosh. Almost at once, the steel plates of the car's interior started to glow a dull purple. The temperature soared. In a flash they were sweating like pigs, their shirts black with perspiration. 'They're gonna burn us alive!' the driver shrieked.

'Shut up!' McLeod bellowed. 'Keep control of yourself, man . . . Gunner, fire smoke.'

'Smoke, sir?'

'Get on with it, man, we're going out of the escape hatch. Move now!'

The driver and the gunner moved. Both started firing the smoke dischargers fixed to both sides of the burning turret. The cartridges sailed into the air, fell once more and exploded with a slight plop, discharging a cloud of thick black smoke almost immediately.

McLeod waited no longer. Drawing his revolver and leaving it to dangle at his waist by its cord, he dropped to the floor of the armoured car, its steel plates now very hot to the touch. He thanked God that this particular car had been modified just on the outbreak of war, when it had received a new Rolls Royce engine and transmission. At the same time, the mechanics had fitted a tank-type escape hatch on the bottom of the vehicle. Now that hatch was going to be the only means of escape from this death trap. Feverishly, feeling all thumbs, McLeod worked on the big screw which kept the hatch in place. Inside the car, the heat was tremendous now, and he could hear their assailant, coughing and spluttering in the sudden smokescreen, sloshing more petrol on the car's hull to keep the fire blazing. McLeod cursed. The plate was proving damned stubborn. Poor maintenance, he told himself angrily, praying at the same time that the smokescreen would last long enough to cover them as they emerged from the car.

Then the last screw gave. He waited no longer. 'Come on, lads!' he cried above the crackle of the flames outside. 'Bale out . . . *gildy!*' They needed no urging. Panicked and streaming with sweat, they pushed by the kneeling McLeod, who felt like some ship's skipper, only ready to abandon ship himself when all his crew had already done so. One by one, they slipped through the hole, fell to the ground and wiggled their way under the burning armoured car. Now it was McLeod's turn. He was much older than his crew, and now he felt his years as he twisted and forced his body awkwardly through the escape hatch. With a gasp, he dropped to the ground, one hand seeking the dangling pistol, for already he could hear the snap and crack of small-arms fire, which might mean his escapees were running into trouble.

He crawled forward, mind racing furiously. He guessed that his crew would have headed round the bend, where the other armoured car was positioned. It would be the obvious thing for them to do. He guessed, too, that the Iraqi assailants would be waiting for anyone else coming from underneath the burning car and heading in the same direction. What was he to do?

He hesitated a mere second. It was too hot to stay underneath the car much longer. Already there was the stink of burning oil from the transmission. It would be only seconds before the engine went up. Now, McLeod realized, it was a matter of timing. If he could wriggle free in that same moment when the armoured car went up and the attackers would reel back, he might well just do it. He started to count off the seconds. '*One . . . two . . . three . . .*' Next moment he was pulling himself out between the rear wheels, revolver in his hand, firing as he did so.

An Iraqi standing there, axe at the ready to slice off his head, went reeling, clutching his shattered chest. Another appeared from the smoke. McLeod fired without aiming. He went down too, blood jetting in a bright red arc from his left shoulder, weapon dropping from suddenly nerveless fingers. Then McLeod was on his feet, as the car exploded, and was pelting for the shelter of the rocks, from which the Iraqis had originally attacked. Next moment he was stumbling and slipping down the steep hillside beyond, to land in a battered, bruised fall at its base, all alone, with not an Iraqi, or anyone else for that matter, in sight.

Three

The Vulture crouched in his 'senior officer's latrine', which was guarded, when he wasn't using it, by an armed sentry. It was an old oil drum from the French plane which had brought them from Syria to this awful desert wilderness. With his pants around his skinny ankles, he held the paper in one hand, and in the other his service pistol, to fight off the rats and the desert mice which swarmed everywhere ever since they had set up the camp two days before.

The Vulture was in a bad mood. He had dysentery again and there was still no news of von Dodenburg's missing First Company – and without their strength, he wasn't going to risk Wotan in any desert attack, armed as his men were with only their small arms. They didn't even possess mortars to give them any added firepower. In essence, Wotan was no better armed than the slovenly, bearded Iraqi Army men who were supposed to guard the SS and eventually lead them to join the rest of the Iraqi brigade besieging the Tommy base in the hills.

The Vulture groaned as he was assailed by another spasm, his guts cramped, as if being squeezed in a steel vice. The waterboy – pretty in a dirty sort of way, the Vulture couldn't help thinking, though he didn't like the silver circles in the Iraqi's cropped hair, which indicated that he suffered from ringworm as well as the usual head lice – hurried forward and offered him the cigarette he was smoking. The Vulture knew it contained some sort of drug the locals used to ease pain, but despite the boy's winning smile, he declined the offer. It wouldn't do for the CO of SS Assault Battalion Wotan to be seen smoking drugged cigarettes by his men, though most of his men, who were suffering too from what they called the 'thin shits', were probably smoking them.

Still the dirty little Iraqi boy continued to smile winningly. He tucked his cigarette away inside his dirty robe and then opened it to reveal his penis. He rubbed it, licking his lips as he did so. '*Du . . . willst?*' he asked in his newly acquired German. 'Very good.'

The Vulture pointed his pistol at him and snapped before he was overcome by yet another spasm, '*Hau ab! Take off, schnell!*'

The little boy got the message and, still smiling in that winning manner of his, wandered off to the main tented camp, leaving the Vulture to sweat and groan, his monocle clouded with sweat. Some time later, the pain eased and the spasms ceased, though the Vulture wondered for how long. He decided, as he cleaned himself, that he'd keep close to his thunderbox; it wouldn't do for him to be caught short. So he called the young soldier who was guarding his personal latrine and ordered him to take up his post once more, commanding, 'Ensure that no one enters but myself, and see that the latrine is ready for instant occupation. Is that clear, sentry?'

'Yessir!' the sentry replied, too frightened of the Vulture to even be amused by the CO's predicament. '*Zu Befehl, Obersturmbannführer.*' And he clicked to attention.

For an instant the Vulture hesitated, as if he wasn't sure he should take a chance and go back to his tent; after all, it was fifty metres away from his personal thunderbox. Then he decided he'd have to take that chance if he was going to get any work done this day. Cautiously, taking very short tight steps, the ugly officer, with his gross nose and mottled face, set off back to his 'HQ'.

Hauptsturmführer Dietz, Wotan's adjutant, was waiting for him there, his slacks stained brown where his dysentery had caught up with him before he had time to pull his pants down. Vulture, hard man that he was, had no sympathy for his adjutant, but Dietz was a good officer, so he said, 'You too, eh?'

'Yessir. Thin shits. Give a little cough and you've a pantsful.

89

Scheisse, what a country! Leave it to the British and their tame niggers, I say.' He shook his big cropped head.

'My sentiments exactly,' the Vulture agreed and sat down – carefully. 'Anything to report?'

'Nothing from the niggers in Baghdad yet, sir.' Dietz's face brightened a little. 'But we have got a prisoner.'

'Prisoner?'

'Yes, some sort of ancient Tommy the buggers brought in half an hour ago. Caught him when they blew up his armoured car.'

'Does he speak German? I'll talk to him if he does.'

'You know the Tommies, sir. Arrogant swine. They don't talk any other lingo than their own. Think everyone understands English. But there's that Indian sergeant from Lieutenant Singh's lot who speaks some German and English. He could do the interpreting, if you wished, sir. Sorry, sir—' Dietz's face turned a sudden white. 'Have to rush, sir . . . the frigging thin shits again . . .' Already undoing his belt and breathing very hard, Dietz rushed out of the tent, heading for the latrine, with the Vulture shouting after him, 'Salute, man . . . salute, d'you hear?'

Five minutes later, escorted by the tall Indian sergeant and a couple of Wotan troopers, who looked at the captive as if he were some sort of curiosity, Squadron Leader McLeod was pushed into the Vulture's HQ tent.

His face was swollen from the beating the Iraqis had given him on capture, and he sensed that a couple of his ribs were broken – there was sharp stabbing pain in his right side every time he moved awkwardly. But McLeod was taking everything in through his swollen eye slits all the same. He knew that he had to note everything and anything for when he escaped. For, despite his present situation and physical condition, he was determined to do so. Now that he was in the hands of the Germans – even though they belonged to Hitler's elite, the SS, with their notorious record for wholesale butchery – he knew he was relatively safe. Unlike the Iraqis, who might kill him on a whim, the Germans would honour the Geneva Convention.

Now, for the time being, he knew he'd have to give something to the Germans to keep them interested, and at the same time retain control over his person. Once they didn't need him and gave him back to the Iraqis who had captured him, he knew that his fate might well be sealed. So, feigning that he was more seriously injured than he was, he allowed himself to be assisted into the Vulture's tent by the Indian sergeant, who, traitor and renegade though he was, obviously still respected the white officers of the army to which he had once belonged before he had thrown in his lot with the Germans.

The Vulture sized the captive up for a few moments, peering at him through his monocle and praying that his jumpy stomach would behave itself during this interrogation. The Tommy was very old and obviously he had been beaten up pretty badly, which didn't help his looks much. Still, he had a defiant look about him and the Vulture could see from the faded ribbons on his bloodstained khaki drill tunic that he was a veteran of the old war. The Vulture decided he wouldn't waste time on preliminaries, but get down to the serious questions immediately, while the Tommy was still in shock after capture. Besides, he had to worry about his own guts and just how long they'd remain quiet before he had to run for the thunderbox for another bout of the thin shits.

Without wasting any time, the Vulture snapped, as the Indian sergeant tensed, ready to interpret his words, 'You are from the air-force base. Why are you out here?'

Back in the 'old war' in the trenches, McLeod had been used to interrogating prisoners himself. During those terrible four years in the line, he had picked up some German. Now that knowledge was coming in useful, despite it being somewhat rusty. The time taken by the Indian to translate the SS officer's question gave him time to consider his answer. So he replied, having assessed swiftly just how much he could give away and still keep the German, with his monstrous beak of a nose, happy, 'I was ordered to look for you.'

That caught the Vulture by surprise. 'How did you know about us?' he rasped.

'Intelligence.' That, McLeod thought, was a blanket expression which might save more revealing explanations.

'I see. And what did your intelligence tell you to expect?'

'A German infantry unit come to help the Iraqi rebels. But, naturally, not an SS formation.'

The Vulture was vaguely pleased. He gave McLeod a careful smile and, in the manner of people who are self-satisfied or flattered, he revealed more than he should have done. 'Yes, I'm sure you didn't expect to have SS Assault Battalion Wotan deposited on your doorstep, what.'

Even the Indian sergeant translating was a little shocked that the German had revealed the name of the formation just like that, but he translated all the same without protest. Indian that he was, he knew that white sahibs, even German ones, had strange ways of their own, not comprehensible to any normal Indian.

'No, sir, unfortunately I didn't,' McLeod replied, telling himself that officers like this SS colonel shouldn't be allowed to interrogate prisoners. He gave away more information than he received. But the Vulture was unaware that he had given away his unit's identity. Pleased with himself, he said, 'Now, I am not going to waste any more time on you, prisoner. I'm going to ask you an important question in a simple way, and I expect a simple answer.' He looked severely at the pale-faced Scot, who looked to him to be on his last legs, an ideal candidate for intimidation. 'If you don't answer it satisfactorily, I must warn you that I may have to give you back to the Iraqis – and I don't think they will be as gentle with you as we Germans.'

McLeod winced and the pain was genuine this time. He knew he wouldn't be able to stand too much punishment from the rebels. So, how was he going to answer the Vulture's question and not give too much away? He tensed and waited for the Indian sergeant to interpret it.

'It is about your base,' the Vulture said. 'We know about your effectives. What we don't know is the number of combat aircraft you possess.'

He stared hard at the prisoner. 'Tell me that number. Hurry please.' The Vulture bit his bottom lip. His stomach was beginning to gurgle once more, like a drain emptying, and he knew it wouldn't be long before he had to rush again for his thunderbox.

McLeod hesitated while the Indian translated. What should he do? Lie or tell the truth? In the end he lied. For the time being, the lie would save him from the damned Iraqis, and by the time the Huns found out that he'd misled them, he might well be dead or safe back at base, where they couldn't touch him. 'I'd say somewhere in the region of two hundred planes of all types,' he answered boldly, looking the Vulture straight in the eye.

'Two hundred!' the Vulture echoed in astonishment. 'As many as that? Great crap on the Christmas tree, I didn't think—' He never finished his sentence. He sensed the urgent need to run for his latrine. Without another word, he grabbed his service pistol and ran for it, leaving the Indian sergeant and McLeod to stare after him in bewilderment, until the latter said, 'Well, Sergeant, what now?'

The Indian, who had obviously not believed him, looked concerned. He lowered his voice and looked hard at the Iraqis who had captured McLeod and beaten him up, and who were now smoking their drugged cigarettes once more. He said, 'Shhh. If I were you, I'd leave here – *soon.*'

McLeod was so shocked by the renegade's words that he heard himself say in bewilderment, 'Thank you for the advice, Sergeant. I think . . . you're right.'

Four

Some fifty miles away from Wotan's camp, another group of SS troopers, the ill-fated survivors of von Dodenburg's First Company, felt the same urgent need to escape. It was three days now since they had fallen in with what Lieutenant Singh called the 'hill people' of the border area, and still there was no sign that the nomadic tribesmen were going to release them or enable them to get into contact with their own people in Baghdad.

It had been early on the evening of the first night of their march eastwards that they had stumbled into the ragged filthy nomads. They had been resting in the shelter of some desert scrub and camel thorn when the sentry had alerted them to the approach of a small band of tall, rangy men with dark flashing eyes and great beaks of noses, riding a collection of broken-down mules and flea-bitten camels. Behind them on foot came their heavily laden womenfolk, clad in black, veiled to the eyes and bearing baskets or pots on their heads.

Von Dodenburg had thrown up his glasses immediately and had surveyed the little caravan, noting immediately that, behind the newcomers, there was another bunch, armed to the teeth and unburdened by women on foot and their scraggy dirty children.

'What do you make of them, Singh?' he had asked the Indian, noting that the second group looked pretty fearsome. There was murder and treachery written all over their tanned leathery faces. They were definitely killers.

'Hill people,' he had answered. 'Nomads from both sides of the border. They owe allegiance to no one, only their tribal chiefs, I've been told.'

A little way behind the officers, Schulze commented, 'They've got mugs only a mother would trust. Look at that arsehole, Matz. The one with the lance, that knife on a stick.' He indicated a skinny rider with a knife scar down the side of his swarthy face. The wound had twisted his right eye so it looked in that direction, as if he were permanently watching for an attack from that quarter. 'Wouldn't like to meet that shite-heel on a dark night.'

Matz agreed solemnly. Unfortunately they were all fated to meet the scar-faced killer on a dark night: that same one, to be exact. It had been an hour after the nomads had seemingly gone their own way, having trailed von Dodenburg's survivors for most of that long day. Von Dodenburg had decided that the time had come to let his weary men rest and enjoy what little food they had left, near a small watercourse they had found, which von Dodenburg had thought was a sign of luck, for they had already exhausted the water they had brought with them from the wreck. They had begun to settle down for the night when it happened.

Suddenly, startlingly, there had been the thunder of many hoofs, interspersed by wild cries and oaths. Out of the evening gloom, the nomads had come charging, ancient rifles blazing, the scar-faced giant waving his lance at the head of the attack. One of the reinforcements on sentry duty had brought up his carbine to fire at him. The boy hadn't a chance. Next moment the giant had skewered him with his lance, lifting him right off his feet before he slid to the ground, dead before he had hit it.

A moment later, the attackers were right in among the surprised Wotan troopers, kicking over their stacked rifles, aiming blows at the uncovered heads of those who attempted to fight back with their bayonets. Here and there troopers tried to run for it, while the mass were pressed back against the rocks, surrendering now, for they had nothing to fight with. They didn't get far. The nomads raced after the fugitives, laughing crazily, waving their weapons about their heads, as if this was the greatest of sports – hunting their fellow humans.

Von Dodenburg got off a last shot before his pistol was

smashed from his hand. One of the riders' mounts reared up in the air, its front hoofs flailing wildly in its death agonies. It rolled to one side and crashed to the ground, smashing into the animal behind, so that it, too, went to the ground in a crazy melee of hoofs and dust and a dying rider. A moment afterwards, Lieutenant Singh commanded, 'Cease firing . . . cease firing . . . It's no use. They've got us. No more blood-shed. I'll take care of this, men . . . *Cease firing!*'

That had been three days before, and although Singh had explained to an angry von Dodenburg, consumed with impatience to get back to the Wotan, that the nomads lived by raiding and kidnapping, selling their captives to the highest bidder, neither the French, the Iraqi rebels nor their own people in Baghdad seemed inclined to pay for their release. As he stated, 'But you must have patience, Captain von Dodenburg. These are a nomadic people who are not in a hurry. Their way of life doesn't encourage it.'

Just as von Dodenburg's patience was running thin, neither Sergeant Schulze nor his running mate, the 'Bavarian barn-shitter', Corporal Matz, was too happy with the situation either. It wasn't that they wanted to get back into action. They were more interested in the old hare's main interests in life: fire-water and fornication. As Schulze complained to Matz on the morning of the third day, when Fatima, the fat cook who attended to their culinary needs, dumped the usual mutton and peppermint tea in their food bowls, 'Cast yer glassy optic on it, will yer, Matz. Frigging sheep's arse and Tommy piss *again*. What I'd give for a nice bowl of fart soup with a fat turd inside it.' He meant the typical German Army pea soup, complete with sausage.

Obviously believing the big sergeant was praising her food, Fatima smiled winningly at him with the one eye she could reveal from beneath her black hood.

Schulze shook his head at her. 'It's no use looking at me like that, Fatima – all goo-goo eyes and the like. I'll never be able to pleasure you in a month o' Sundays. Your lot'd dock my dick in zero-comma-nothing seconds, old girl.'

Fatima's smile, hidden as it was, must have broadened even

more, for that single eye, outlined by *kohl*, beamed even more.

Next to Matz, Schulze fiddled with his mutton stew, pulling out the usual eye and staring at it with disgust, while Matz ventured: 'Why do you think they dress their women up like that? You can't see their tits or pins or anything. It ain't natural, is it, Schulze?'

Schulze, who regarded himself as an authority on most things foreign, let the eye drop back into his stew with a plop, and pontificated, 'It's their religion, Matzi. If they can't see the women's bits and pieces, they don't got randy like yer normal white man. It's a kind of contra— con—. *Scheisse*, you know what I mean, Matzi.'

'But they do have kids,' Matz objected. 'Lots of the little nipple-nippers.'

'Perhaps they're only allowed to do it on their holy days,' Schulze suggested, 'like it's written in their Bible.'

'Bible!' Matz puffed out his lips in contempt at such ignorance. 'Didn't you ever go to school? The Bible's for Christians like us, not for heathens. They're Muslims, you know. They have what they call the Talmud. It's a big thing their priests carry around, chanting all the time. I've seen it somewhere or other.'

'Oh,' Schulze said. 'Well, you Catholic Bavarian barnshitters'll know all about that sort o' stuff. Up north where I come from, Matzi, we don't go in for religion much. We're more into beer and schnapps.'

'Sergeant Schulze!' Von Dodenburg's incisive voice brought the high-level theological discussion to an abrupt end. 'I want your opinion.'

'Sir.' Schulze came to his feet, dropping his spoon back into his mutton stew, causing one of the sheep's eyes to pop and fall to the ground to stare up at him, as if in mild surprise at this sudden transportation from water to earth. 'On what, sir?'

'Our chances of making a break for it from this dump,' von Dodenburg answered. 'We've been here long enough. Lieutenant Singh is getting us nowhere with these savages.'

Schulze frowned. 'We've got no weapons, sir,' he said.

97

'They're either using them themselves or they've got them tucked away somewhere in one of those filthy huts of theirs. And I don't fancy our chances if we've got no weapons against them.'

'Yessir,' Matz chimed in. 'That wall-eyed bugger o' theirs'd dearly like to stick that lance of his up one of our arses.'

Now it was von Dodenburg's turn to frown. 'I take your point. But we can't stay here for ever.'

'I know, sir. I'm with yer. What wouldn't I give for some decent German fodder and, with luck, a good glass of Munich suds.' He licked his parched lips, as if he could already taste a litre of Bavarian beer about to take the delightful voyage to his stomach. 'A poor stubble-hopper like me could die happy if he could sink one of those behind his collar stud.'

Von Dodenburg forced a smile. 'All right, see if you can discover where they're hiding the rest of our weapons, especially the machine pistols. A couple of those in our hands and we'd soon settle the beggars' hash for them.'

'You can say that again, sir,' Matz said heartily, as Schulze tossed the rest of his mutton stew over his shoulder with, 'We'll do it, and I'm not going to swallow no more of Fatima's frigging sheep's arse either.'

Von Dodenburg could see that his two old hares were determined enough, though he hadn't the faintest idea who Fatima was. Knowing Matz and Schulze, he guessed that if she was a woman, they'd soon use her to their own advantage – and then some.

It was later that same morning that Lieutenant Singh, watched suspiciously by the giant Iraqi with the twisted eye, disclosed the latest stage of his talks with the nomads. 'Von Dodenburg, sir,' he said, a smile on his handsome face. 'Things are moving at last.'

'How?'

'They're going to get us to Baghdad.'

'What do you say?' von Dodenburg queried, with a sense of mounting excitement.

'They've been in contact with the representatives of this chap Raschid Ali who raised the flag of revolt against the

98

English colonialist swine last week. The people in Baghdad are apparently prepared to pay a ransom for us when we're brought to the nearest road-head, some thirty or so kilometres away from here. From thence we'll be forwarded to Baghdad and in due course returned to SS Assault Battalion Wotan. Now, what do you say to that, eh?' he added enthusiastically.

'I'd say splendid, Lieutenant Singh. You've done a fine job. Save for one thing.'

'And what's that?'

'Can we trust them?' Von Dodenburg looked at the wall-eyed Iraqi's face over Singh's shoulder. If he'd ever seen murder written across a man's face, it was on his.

'But why shouldn't we trust him and his fellows? I mean, they have everything to gain, haven't they, sir, by handing us back to the authorities.'

'Have they?'

'How do you mean, sir?'

Von Dodenburg lowered his voice, though he knew the wall-eyed chief didn't understand. 'We've been subjected to his blackmail ever since they captured us, haven't we, Singh?'

'I suppose you could call it that, sir.'

'I do. Now, why should he give up the goose that lays the golden egg just like that? He could take us to the road-head to meet the Baghdad people, collect his ransom money and then refuse to give us up to them. I wouldn't put it past the big bastard for one moment.'

Singh frowned. 'But do you think he'd do that, sir?'

'Of course I do. This whole operation is a mess, totally messed up and badly planned. To my way of thinking, the only people who are going to profit from it are those like that wall-eyed scum. He has no loyalty to any cause but his own.'

Singh absorbed the information for a moment or two before saying, 'Well, if you're right, Captain von Dodenburg, what are we going to be able to do about it?'

Von Dodenburg had his answer ready. 'This!' he snapped, his lean face hard and arrogant. 'Shaft him, before he shafts us.' And the young SS officer made his point quite clear with a gesture, as if he were thrusting a knife into the guts of an enemy, right up to the hilt. Twenty metres away, the wall-eyed giant looked suddenly very grim, as if, though he didn't understand von Dodenburg's words, he certainly understood his intentions.

Five

McLeod prepared well for his escape. He wanted the Germans to regard him as a broken-down old man whose injuries made it virtually impossible for him to think of escaping. Twice when the guards had brought food to his tent he had coughed blood before he could eat it, and then rejected the meal, though he was hungry enough. The blood had come from biting his lips just as he had heard the guards approaching. That last night, he had coughed a great deal, interspersed with moaning, so that twice the sentry had come to tell him to shut his moaning up and ask what was the matter with him. His reply had been in German: '*Meine Rippen – die sind kaputt.*' Thereafter there had been a noticeable lessening of the guards' interest in him, and one of the younger ones had offered him a Bayer aspirin to lessen the supposed pain.

Still, McLeod had been very surprised when the Indian sergeant who had done the translating had made an appearance, and with a doleful face had moaned, 'I am a bad man, Sahib. I have betrayed the King Emperor – I, a sergeant in the 1st Bengal Rifles.' For a moment McLeod had thought the middle-aged Indian NCO might well begin to cry. Instead the Indian had looked furtively from left to right, and then from beneath his tunic he had produced, first a small Italian pistol, then a water bottle and a bar of chocolate. Hastily he had pressed the gifts into a surprised McLeod's hands, whispering, 'You go, Sahib – it is all I can give you. God go with you.' And with that he was gone, leaving McLeod again to wonder at the strangeness of the Indian character.

That pre-dawn he made his break. The tented camp was sunk in a heavy sleep. Even the Iraqi dogs were silent,

101

something for which McLeod was very grateful. The only sounds were the snores of the enemy and the soft rustle of the wind in the camel scrub. Moving with exaggerated slowness, he crept by the sentry who was asleep on a box, head on his chest, rifle propped against the side of the box. McLeod told himself the poor young bugger was in for a real rollicking in the morning when it was discovered that his prisoner had done a bunk while he had snored.

He moved on. Here and there in the Iraqi horse lines, a nervous animal tossed its mane and whinnied. But the movement of the horses caused no reaction in the camp. The camp slept on and McLeod reasoned anyone hearing agitation of the animals would attribute it to the storm which was clearly brewing. For the dawn sky was starting to flush an ugly white, and the wind was rising steadily. Under other circumstances, McLeod would have cursed. For, old Iraq hand that he was, he knew what was on its way: a sandstorm. But now the storm would come at an ideal time for him. It would be one devil of a job working against it, but at least it would cover his tracks and make it virtually impossible for any pursuers to follow him with any accuracy.

Half an hour later, the storm had still not come, but the air was now virtually impossible to breathe. It was furnace-hot, with the sky the colour of wood smoke. Not a breath of wind stirred, the dawn breeze had vanished altogether and the sun itself was like a copper penny glimpsed at the bottom of a green-scummed pond.

The going was hell. Still McLeod knew he couldn't let up. By now his departure would have been noticed, and he knew well that the ugly CO of the German SS troops would try his damnedest to find him – he couldn't afford to let his position be revealed to the British, in case the fugitive managed to contact his own troops.

Now the hot air seared his lungs like a flame from a blowtorch. His uniform was black with sweat. Beads of perspiration streamed down his forehead and stung and blinded his faded blue eyes. Still he staggered on, that tremendous heat wringing the sweat out of his lean body like a washerwoman squeezing out a wet sponge. Even the sand was against him. It rose in small powdery clouds about his boots, the fine particles stinging his bare knees like sharp painful nicks from a thousand razors.

Time and time again, he cursed angrily, knowing that anger against these cruel elements would keep him going. Anger would make him refuse to submit, for once he sat down, he knew he'd be doomed. He wouldn't get up again. Cursing and carefully rationing himself to one sip of water from the bottle the Indian sergeant had given him, staggering now and again like a drunk, he kept on going, knowing that the worst was still to come.

But when that worst came, it came just in time. Just as he had become dimly aware of the faint shouts behind him which indicated that his pursuers had caught up with him, there was a strange humming sound. He had heard it before, but, numb as he was, and almost at the end of his tether, he couldn't identify it immediately. He turned, his head working slowly, as if on rusty springs. He saw the tiny black dots behind him which were the enemy. But it was the great whirling spinning top of sand and dust reaching right up to the sky that really caught his attention.

Moments later, the tornado of sand struck him at a speed of fifty miles per hour. In a flash, all was dirty yellow, whirling, choking sand. Its particles were razor sharp. They slashed and cut the skin. They penetrated his worn khaki uniform. They ripped cruelly at his flesh, making him yelp with pain. Frantically he attempted to stay upright in that howling, whirling darkness, everything else blackened out. He knew he had to stay stable. If he let go, he'd be blown for miles into the desert, perhaps never to be found again.

He sank to his knees and, groping blindly, found a patch of firm camel scrub. He clutched at it desperately. It held and then he began what seemed an interminable fight with Nature itself. Time and time again that tremendous wind, howling like ten thousand banshees, buffeted his old skinny body. It slammed into him with all its fury, as if it were determined to wipe him off the face of the earth. He cried out for mercy.

103

None came. 'Will it never end?' he called, mouth filling instantly with choking sand. Desperately, he clung to the camel thorn as that terrible wind tried to sweep him away. God, it was impossible!

Then it was over. As abruptly as the sandstorm had started, it ended. One moment the world was all chaos. The next the obscene howling of that awful wind had been replaced by a soft dirge-like moan which, in its turn, was replaced a few seconds afterwards by a gossamer-light breeze which gave way to nothing, leaving behind a kind of loud echoing silence.

For what seemed ages, McLeod didn't react. He continued to cling to the camel thorn, covered in sand, as if he were already interred in some kind of desert grave. Then, finally, he started to stir. His free hand broke through the sand. With its help he clawed the sand from his eyes and mouth, coughing and spluttering. He licked his lips. They looked like bloody slashes across his sand-caked face. Finally he was ready. He looked behind him. His pursuers had vanished. In their place was a lone figure in khaki, his rifle aimed right at McLeod's chest. Slowly, very slowly, he started to raise his hands . . .

Ten kilometres away, an angry Vulture made his decision. He faced up to Dietz, who he held responsible for the escape of their prisoner, and barked, 'We have no other alternative, Dietz. We're moving.'

The unhappy adjutant, who knew the Vulture of old, and how he could make things decidedly unpleasant for those who had offended him, said, 'It will be difficult, sir. We have no transport, for a start.'

'Get some,' the Vulture snapped. 'I have waited long enough for our people in Baghdad to make a decision. This whole damned operation is ill-conceived, but I'm not going to go along with it any longer. I am not risking my battalion any longer. Baghdad must supply us with wheels to get us away from this hellhole – and, Dietz, I don't give a damn about what these niggers –' he meant the Iraqis – 'think. We are German soldiers, soldiers of the Führer himself. I don't think he would be happy if he knew how we were being wasted in this godforsaken wilderness, do you, Dietz?'

There was no answer to that, and an unfortunate Dietz knew it. He clicked to attention and snapped, '*Jawohl Obersturmbannführer! Wird gemacht!*'

Half an hour later, Dietz, hovering impatiently next to the battalion's radio operator, was listening to him as he signalled the Vulture's urgent wish to the German embassy in Baghdad, while a delighted Air Commodore Jeeves, too, listened as the senior intelligence officer broke the coded message bit by bit, exclaiming at periodic intervals, 'We've got the bugger by God! We've got 'em! They're on the run!'

Jeeves knew – when he had pondered the Vulture's message for a while over a 'chota peg' at the mess, while, in the hills, Iraqi artillery had commenced firing once again – that he hadn't sufficient infantry to attempt to intercept these Germans whenever they started for Baghdad. His local levies would be no good against trained German soldiers. Nor could he strip his defence around the air base. The Iraqis in the hills might get it into their heads to attack once it was clear to them that they were likely not to meet much British opposition. In reality, Jeeves told himself, his only really effective means of attack on these Germans would be his make-shift bomber and fighter-bomber aircraft.

He guessed German infantry would have little in the way of anti-aircraft weapons. All the same, slow-moving antiquated aircraft, such as his were, manned by untrained crews, would still be fairly easy targets for mass infantry rifle and machine-gun fire. And once he had lost his aircraft, then the great base would be virtually defenceless against any serious attack by the Iraqis in the hills.

He frowned. Behind the bar, the white-jacketed mess steward asked helpfully, 'Another peg, sir?'

Absently Jeeves nodded. Through the open door, he could see a couple of the trainee pilots waffling on excitedly about the mission against the Iraqis which they had flown the previous afternoon. Their talk was full of old-timers' slang – 'wizard prang' . . . 'gave the old kite all she'd got' . . . 'no stooging around, you know, old bean . . .' They sounded as if they had been in service since the days of Lord Trenchard and the old Royal Flying Corps. Instead they were a couple of fresh-faced kids who couldn't have been a day older than nineteen. He looked at them for a minute or so, as they sipped their beer from – naturally – silver tankards, as if they were real old hands, and told himself they wouldn't see out the year before they got the chop. Could he shorten their lives even more by sending them on a new mission against the Huns somewhere out there in the desert?

The mess steward brought him his second 'chota peg', and he took a hefty drink of it which made him cough. He knew there was little time for pity or sentiment in wartime. It was always the young and the best who died first; it had always been thus. But what of the future, when the war was over and the young and the best were all dead? His frown deepened. What the hell was he going to do, dammit?

It was then that the MO and his medical orderly helped the pathetic wreck of a man into the bar. His face was hollowed out by privation and torn by camel thorn, so much so that a startled Jeeves didn't recognize him until the wreck croaked, 'I wouldna mind a wee dram mysen, Commodore, if you're pushing the boat out.'

Jeeves nearly fell off the barstool. 'Good God!' he exclaimed. 'It's you, McLeod. We'd given you up for dead, man.'

McLeod gave a weak smile, as the medical officer helped him to sit down. Ten minutes later, after yet another dram, the exhausted squadron leader had made up Jeeves' mind for him. The raid on the Germans, suicidal or not, would go ahead . . .

BOOK FOUR

Disaster

One

On the same day that the Vulture received his signal from the German Legation in Baghdad that a convoy of Iraqi Army trucks would carry his men out of the desert to Baghdad, where they would be reformed and supplied with heavy weapons before transferring to the Iraqi Brigade besieging RAF Habbaniyah, von Dodenburg made his own decision. But, unlike the Vulture, who would be heading east with what remained of SS Wotan, he would go west.

As he confided to Matz and Schulze, whom he hoped would steal him the machine pistols they would need for their escape, 'I've had enough of this damned country. Let the Iraqis do what they like. My job is to save what's left of my First Company.'

'But why west, sir?' Matz had queried.

'Because that's the way our captors won't expect us to go, Corporal.'

Schulze beamed. 'If I may say so, sir, that's smart thinking.'

'You may,' von Dodenburg had replied sardonically. 'Now, let me see you do some smart thinking, you big rogue, and get me some firepower. We've got to be armed, that's for certain.'

'It will be done, sir,' Schulze said solemnly. 'Me and Matzi's got a plan. When we going?'

'As soon as possible. Tonight if you can get those weapons. And see the men take a full water bottle with them, and something – anything – that'll sustain them till we reach the Syrian frontier. Dates, some of that flat bread the nomads eat, anything that they can save from the day's rations. All right, get on with it. I want to work out my plan.' And with that he had vanished, watched, unknown to the three Wotan men, by Lieutenant Singh, whose handsome brown face looked worried.

'My piles are getting frigging piles, honest, Schulzi,' Matz moaned as they crouched there in the cold light of the full moon, watching the nomads' huts. It was half an hour now since Fatima had smuggled herself out of her father's hut into that one inhabited by the wall-eyed giant. Still nothing had happened, and Schulze had commented impatiently, 'Slow buggers aren't they, these towel-heads? Wouldn't take Frau Schulze's handsome son long to get a diamond-cutter and give her a piece of stiff German salami that'd make her eyes pop, believe you me.'

'Go on,' Matz sneered softly. 'A limp-tail like you. She'd be panting for a bit o' my Bavarian schnitzel though . . .' He stopped short. 'Look, they're beginning to dance the mattress polka!'

Matz was right. From inside the hut came the sound of heavy panting and giggles of delight.

Schulze wasted no more time. 'Come on!' he hissed. 'Let's have a look-see.' Noiselessly, for such a big man, he crept to the rear of the makeshift hut and peered inside through a gap in the material. By the light of a wildly flickering candle, he could just see a naked Fatima balanced on top of an equally naked wall-eyed giant, pumping herself up and down with obvious delight, her mighty breasts quivering like great white puddings. 'Will you cast yer glassy orbs on that, Matzi,' he whispered.

Matz was so overcome by the sight that he crossed himself and hissed, 'Holy strawsack, Schulzi, all that meat and no potatoes. That black gown of hers hid a lot.'

Schulze swallowed hard as, carried away by a frenzy of wild passion, the big woman rode the giant so hard that her nipples started to slap her chin loudly.

Next to Matzi, he whispered in an awed voice, 'The way she's going at it, yer'd think she'd do him an injury.'

Schulze tore his gaze from that scene of crazy sexual abandon and sighed, 'Great crap on the Christmas tree, Matzi,

I only wish she'd do me an injury like . . . Come on, let's go and find those frigging popguns.' Whispering to himself just how hard the poor average stubble-hopper's lot was, he led Matz to the attached hut, where the wall-eyed giant had secured the machine pistols he had taken from the Wotan troopers when they had been forced to surrender. Minutes later, they were on their way back to their rendezvous point with von Dodenburg and the rest, including a surprised Lieutenant Singh, who had been roused from his sleep to be told they were breaking out, laden with four machine pistols apiece and ammunition. Behind them, the wall-eyed giant and the monstrous naked Fatima were now engaged in some complicated, if delightful, dog-like sex, while the rest of the nomad camp seemingly slept on.

Von Dodenburg led the way, with the men armed with the machine pistols to the front and rear of the thin column. The moon was out and he could see the land to the west stretching out in front of him. He thought it a vast dead land in which nothing grew – harsh, cruel and inhospitable. He frowned abruptly, feeling that somehow this land saw him and his troopers as intruders. It was an odd sensation. He shuddered, fighting back the strange sensation that there was something out there watching them. 'Idiot,' he cursed to himself. 'Like a stupid old dame, thinking that there are robbers under her bed.' He told himself he should be glad that he was clearing out of the place at last. Iraq was a country that he personally didn't want to see again, and he felt sure that the rest of his men felt the same.

Lieutenant Singh, however, didn't share his sentiments. As they headed westwards, strung out in a long file, hands dug deep into their pockets for warmth, heads bent into the protection of their collars against the night cold, Singh said, 'I hope you will forgive me, von Dodenburg, but I hope you know what you're doing.'

'How do you mean?' von Dodenburg asked.

'I mean, the Führer himself ordered this operation. Now you're abandoning it and returning to the uncertainties of French Syria.'

Singh's tone, as it often did, annoyed von Dodenburg. He snapped back, 'I can assure you that I do know what I'm doing. What can I and a handful of men, virtually without weapons, do here, I ask you? No, Singh, my first concern is my men. I've got to save them from this terrible shitty place.'

Singh grunted something and their conversation died away to nothing. For a few moments, von Dodenburg considered the Indian's words, telling himself that, despite his charm and intelligence, Singh was a queer bird; he seemed much more enthusiastic about this Iraq mission than his own troopers. Then he dismissed the young handsome officer and concentrated on the way ahead.

The night air was clear and invigorating, the going was easy, with firm sand, and there was something soothing now about the vastness of the silver-velvet sky. He told himself he was going to pull it off. For a change, ever since they had left Athens, luck was on their side; they'd reach the Syrian border all right, he knew that instinctively.

Time passed. The moon now scudded in and out of the clouds. Every so often black shadows swept silently across the desert. Here and there the Wotan troopers spotted stunted bushes as the moon reappeared, and, for a moment, took them for men waiting silently for them to come closer before opening fire. And every time, after they saw they'd been fooled, they'd curse themselves for having been taken in, until it happened again. Passing up and down the line to reassure the men, von Dodenburg could understand their feelings. It was now about three hours since they had slipped out of the nomads' camp. By this time, surely, the nomads must have realized they had gone. The question was, would they attempt to pursue the fugitives? After all, the Wotan troopers did represent hard cash to them.

'What do you think?' he asked Schulze and Matz as he came up to them acting as the escapers' rearguard.

Matz chuckled. 'The way Fatima was giving the wall-eyed bugger a bit o' the other, I don't think he'll be getting up as soon, sir. She was really knocking the stuffing out of the ugly bastard.'

'And it wasn't stuffing she was knocking out of him, sir,' Schulze hinted. 'No, sir, I don't think they'll be after us soon. Will we reach the Syrian frontier before they get the digit out of the orifice?'

'I'm hoping so, Schulze. Just after dawn is my guess, if we can keep up this pace.'

'Well then, sir,' Schulze said with new enthusiasm. 'It looks as if we're gonna outrun the towel-heads.'

But Schulze, as he often was, was going to be proved wrong.

'Look, sir,' Singh began.

Von Dodenburg clamped his hand around the Indian's mouth. 'Shut up!' he hissed roughly. 'I can see him.' He bent low and then, using the old soldier's trick, he turned his head to one side and swung it to his front, with his gaze held close to the ground. A moment's pause. Suddenly he looked up. Yes, looming up a lighter black against the background of the night, he saw first one, then two and three men standing motionless there. He frowned. But he *had* expected trouble here, if anywhere. There were two hills covering the trail, and the unknowns had taken up their position on the hill to the right, which gave them access to direct fire on the route below. In short, it was an ideal place for an ambush, if this was what was intended; and somehow von Dodenburg guessed it was.

Slowly he released his grip on Singh's mouth and the latter gasped, 'Nomads?'

'Could be. At all events, I don't think their intentions are particularly honourable. And there are more of them beyond the bluff. I can hear them.'

Surprisingly, Singh didn't seem worried or frightened, just puzzled as to what von Dodenburg might do next. Perhaps he thought a veteran like the young SS captain had encountered situations like this many times before and knew what to do. 'What do we do?' Singh asked.

Under other circumstances, von Dodenburg might have laughed at that '*we*'. Not now. The situation was too serious. With the few weapons he had at his command, he knew he couldn't engage in a full-scale battle. He had to take the enemy

113

by surprise and make it short and, he hoped, sweet. 'No "we",' he answered. '*I.*'

'Sorry,' Singh mumbled. 'I understand.'

Von Dodenburg forgot Singh. He had other things to think about. He looked at the steep hillside to his right, visible for a moment in the fleeting light of the moon. 'What do you think, Schulze?' he asked, as the big NCO came creeping up to where he and Singh crouched.

Schulze sniffed. 'Looks a tough bastard. But me and Matzi here can manage it.'

Matz groaned at the way Schulze was volunteering his services, but Schulze didn't appear to notice.

'All right,' von Dodenburg said. 'This is the drill. We don't want a full-scale fight, we haven't got the strength. I want you two rogues to scatter them, make them think there are more of us than there are.'

'We've only got four mags apiece,' Matz objected. 'We'll soon use them up.'

'Then we'll use them, you little piss pansy,' Schulze sneered. 'Then you can bite the friggers to death with yer teeth. We're ready, sir.'

'Off you go then, Schulze. We'll keep moving slowly forward as if we've seen nothing. They'll concentrate on us, I hope.'

'Don't you worry, sir,' Schulze said. 'We'll see the towelheads off. After all, we're Wotan.'

Von Dodenburg choked. He might well be sending the two old hares off to their deaths. But that fact didn't seem to worry them. They went willingly, even gladly. Where did one find soldiers like these? 'Look after yourselves,' he said thickly. 'Keep your eyes peeled, do you hear?'

'Yessir,' Matz replied. 'Like the proverbial tinned tomatoes.' And with that they had vanished into the darkness.

Two

Digging his toes into the sandy rock, his machine pistol slung across his broad shoulders, Schulze started the ascent. It was more difficult than he had anticipated, especially now that the moon had disappeared beneath the clouds once more. Clinging to the few handholds he could find, till the ends of his fingers were numb with pain and he felt he could hold on no longer, he edged his way, millimetre by millimetre, up the cliff face. Soon, despite the coolness of the night, the sweat was pouring off him. It soaked his uniform, which clung to him unpleasantly and threatened to blind him with sweat time and time again.

Then he hit an easy slope and his progress was quicker. Not for long. He was faced by several metres of murderous camel thorn that tore and ripped and tore at his flesh cruelly. Once, he hung perilously by his fingertips, unable to move due to the thorns which had attached themselves to his torn slacks. Desperately, he twisted and turned for what seemed an age, to free himself from these sharp barbs. As one gave, another lashed out and whipped itself against his tortured body. It took all his will power to prevent himself from crying out loud with the pain from those cruel thorns.

Once, he paused, and could hear the rest of the company advancing towards the pass. To Schulze, hanging there gasping for breath, it seemed they were making a hell of a noise for trained soldiers. But then, he told himself, that was part of the CO's plan. Now he put the toe of his boot in a hold and reached his hand up the sharp edge of the flattish rock just above his head. The foothold gave. For a moment he thought he'd tumble down to the bottom of the steep hill. He didn't.

115

But his hand slipped too. The rock ripped off a fingernail. A wave of almost unbearable pain swept through his body. He thrust his grey face against the dirt. It stifled his cry of agony – just in time.

Next moment he'd made it, to lie face forward on the top, gasping for breath like someone who had just run a great race.

Matz led the way, with legs that felt strangely rubbery. They had unslung their machine pistols and, in the soft purple of the pre-dawn sky, they edged their way to where the enemy, if they were really the enemy, would be waiting for the rest of Wotan's First Company.

To the east, the sky was beginning to flush a dramatic red. Things were being bathed in a warm crimson light, everything sharp, hard, brittle, with the waiting enemy on the hilltop silhouetted a stark black. Ten minutes more and the sun would rise over the horizon and the ground would begin to burn, ridding it of any shadows. But for the time being the two NCOs could still worm their way forward in the patches of blackness, using the 'dead ground' to their advantage.

Out of the side of his mouth, Schulze hissed, 'Get as close as possible, Matzi, and then, when I give you the wire, open up. We're not going to give ourselves away by challenging the towel-heads. They're armed, they're acting suspicious-like; therefore they're for the chop. *Klar?*'

'*Klar.*'

They wriggled on, getting ever closer to the unsuspecting 'towel-heads', whose gaze was concentrated on the Wotan troopers down below as they approached the pass.

To the rear of the waiting lookouts there were others, lying on the ground – perhaps a score of them, some of them holding the halters of their mounts, perhaps to steady them when the firing commenced. Most of them looked half asleep, something for which Schulze was thankful. For his rough-and-ready plan was daring and risky. He and Matz would take the lot of them out, using up all their ammunition to do so. It was chancey, he knew – very. It needed only one stoppage and then the enemy would have them by the short and curlies. But if it worked, it would save casualties among the troopers below, half of whom were totally unarmed.

Now they were within ten metres of the first group of towel-heads. Matz paused and raised his machine pistol. Hastily Schulze stopped him. 'Fire over their heads and hit the swine on—' He stopped abruptly.

Close to them, one of the second group had stirred. In the clear pre-dawn air, the two noncoms could see every detail registering on his dark, hawk-like face. He stared at the two white men crouching there stupidly, as if he couldn't yet work out why they were there. Suddenly his face showed shocked indignation. He opened his mouth to shout a warning, and at the same moment grabbed for his rifle on the ground beside him. He never reached it. 'Try this on for size, arse-with-ears,' Matz cried, and, rising to his knees, loosed off a burst in an instant.

The man reeled back, what looked like a series of red buttonholes stitched the length of his skinny chest. Throwing caution to the wind now, the two NCOs charged, firing from the hip as they did so.

The natives went down on all sides, caught by surprise. Like two Western gunslingers, the two comrades fired from the hip, swinging their machine pistols from side to side murderously. A man ran at them. For some reason he was naked below the waist, boots, unlaced, flapping on his feet. Why he was wearing boots, Schulze neither knew nor cared (later he'd find out to his cost why). He hardly seemed to aim. The half-naked man hit the ground, punching holes in the sand with his clenched fist while the blood spurted from his ripped-open stomach, his shattered intestines sliding to the ground like a steaming grey-green serpent.

Down below, von Dodenburg heard the sudden burst of small-arms fire and knew instinctively what his two rogues had done. They had taken it upon themselves to assault the enemy single-handed, not waiting for him. 'The stupid swine,' he muttered, half in anger, half in admiration. But there was no time to be wasted on recriminations. He had to support the two noncoms the best he could with his two machine pistols and the old hares who had filled their spare socks with sand and were going to use them as clubs. He drew the pistol which Schulze had given him. 'Follow me,' he cried boldly over the angry snap and crackle of small-arms fire coming from above. *'Attack!'*

His Wotan troopers obeyed at once, although they knew the odds were against them. As von Dodenburg started to stumble up the hill at the pass, waving the little popgun, they spread out in attack formation, as if this was a well-armed Wotan infantry company instead of a collection of broken-down, half-starved men, most of them unarmed. *'Alles für Deutschland!'* they yelled, shouting the bold motto of the Black Guards. *'Es lebe der Führer! Adolf Hitler!'*

The enemy up on top were taken by surprise. They had not anticipated an attack from front and rear. They wavered and started to pull back, firing wildly without taking aim, a sure sign of panic, von Dodenburg knew. A native came rushing at him. Surprisingly enough, he was armed with bayonet and rifle like a regular infantryman. Von Dodenburg had no time to ponder the mystery. The native lunged at him. Expertly von Dodenburg parried the thrust with his pistol. Next instant he fired. The impact was so great at that short distance that the native was thrown off his feet and propelled backwards, as if punched by some giant fist. As he ran forward, von Dodenburg kicked him in the side of his face. His head fell to the right with a dry click. He was dead.

A few minutes later, it was over. The ambush, if that was what had been intended, had been a total failure. The top of the hill was a bloodstained shambles: a gory mixture of dead and dying men, scuffed sand, cartridge cases which gleamed like gold in the new sun, the only sound the pleas for mercy from the prisoners, who had gone down on their knees begging not to be shot by their captors.

Ten metres away from where their prisoners were begging for their lives in a language that even Lieutenant Singh, who seemed to speak many languages, couldn't understand, von Dodenburg was caught completely by surprise at the sight of Schulze's prisoner. Just like the other prisoners, he was terrified of his captors, and tears were rolling unheeded down his fat dark face as Schulze prodded him forward, with Matz to the rear, enjoying the bottle of raki, which the two rogues had obviously just taken from their prisoner.

'Caught him hiding over there, sir,' Schulze said. 'He was waiting for us to go before he did a bunk. And he had a bottle of fire water – Matzi, don't guzzle the shitting lot, willyer.'

Von Dodenburg wasn't listening, for the fat prisoner wore a shabby uniform with the stripes of an NCO on his arm. He was wearing some sort of army boots, too, as von Dodenburg now realized most of their prisoners were. 'But he's a soldier,' von Dodenburg managed to stutter. 'Not one of the nomads, as I expected they were.'

'That's right, sir,' Schulze said easily, grabbing the bottle of raki from Matz's unwilling hand. 'He had a regulation kepi, a white one, as well. But I took it from him. I thought he might have some lung torpedoes –' Schulze meant cigarettes – 'hidden in the crown.'

'*A kepi!*' von Dodenburg began, but Singh, who had just made his appearance, beat him to it.

'And that means he's a member of the French Army . . . perhaps from Syria.'

'But we can't have reached the Iraq-Syrian border yet,' von Dodenburg objected.

'I don't think the French take that too seriously,' Singh said. 'It's outlaw country up here. No one pays much attention to the border here, I should think.' He turned to the sobbing NCO and snapped in French, '*Ne pleurez pas, hein. Nous sommes des amis.*'

The prisoner stopped crying immediately and gave them a gold-toothed smile. '*Merci, monsieur.*'

Before anyone could stop him, he darted forward and, seizing a bewildered von Dodenburg's hand, kissed it fervently, as if he would never let go of it again.

Matz shook his head in mock wonder. 'Frogs!' he exclaimed. 'They make love with their tongues and kiss other men's hands like a bunch of frigging warm brothers. What a country!'

The knowledge that they had fought with a patrol of French

119

levies, who were Germany's new allies and had killed far too many of them, placed von Dodenburg in a quandary. 'The French are a people that I do not like greatly,' he explained to Singh, as if the latter would know little of the history of Franco-German relations. 'We've fought each other too often. I had a grandfather killed at Sedan in '70, and my father was badly wounded at Verdun in '16 – and, of course, I fought them myself last year on the Somme. Still, they are our allies, and I don't want to cause trouble. So, what am I going to do? If we cross into Syria, how do I explain this?' With a sweep of his hand he encompassed the prisoners, who he had ordered released, but not allowed to leave their hilltop camp. 'There'd be one hell of a stink if it came out what I'd done with their comrades.'

Singh gave a little laugh. 'Kill them,' he suggested. 'Then the matter will remain secret.'

Von Dodenburg looked at the Indian sharply. Was he joking? He never quite knew with Singh. At times he was ferocious, making such cruel suggestions as he had done with the story of the rat forced up a man's anus. Yet, at the same time, he didn't seem a bloodthirsty person. At least, he had not shown any inclination of that kind so far.

But von Dodenburg had no time to consider the puzzle presented by the handsome young Indian officer any further. For, standing watch on the hilltop, Matz was now shouting, 'Problems, sir . . . Problems. Looks as if the whole of the Frog army's on its way to have a little chat with us . . .'

Three

Von Dodenburg groaned. Slowly he opened his puffed-up eyes. Everything shimmered before his gaze. He closed his eyes again, more swiftly, and felt the electric wave of pain shoot through his battered body.

He counted to three and tried to maintain some sort of discipline over himself by ordering himself, 'Open your eyes, Kuno.' He did so and this time the cell came into view without shaking and trembling, what there was of it, and that wasn't very much. A chair which had been screwed to the concrete floor, a jug of water near the hole which served as a latrine, and the concrete slab on which he now lay, naked as a worm with his bloodstained feet chained to its base. He stifled the groan which came to his swollen lips when he realized just how bad his condition and situation was. It would do no good to bemoan his fate. He had to concentrate on bringing this miserable ordeal to an end. First he must drink something.

Slowly, laboriously, he reached out as far as he could to grab the jug of water next to the latrine hole. His every movement took an effort of naked will power, pain starting up everywhere on his battered, bruised, naked frame. He gritted his teeth and kept going. He had to have a drink. After what seemed an age, he reached the jug. Carefully, very carefully, he started to pull it towards him across the floor, a rat scuttling away in the shadows, frightened by the strange noise. The jug seemed to weigh a ton. He persisted. Finally he had it within drink range. He bent his head over the edge of the concrete sleeping slab, felt the cool rim of the jug and readied his shaking hand for the final movement. Next instant he let the precious jug of water go with an angry curse. It was empty!

He could have burst into tears at the utter base treachery. Before he had fainted, he remembered clearly one of his torturers saying, '*Bon, sale Boche*, there is water in the jug. That's all you're getting . . .' Now they hadn't even left him a cup of the precious liquid. How cruel the French were . . .

The meeting between the Wotan survivors and the men of the French convoy just after the battle of the pass had been frosty from the very start and it was going to become even more frosty. The Citroën half-tracks had stopped some half a kilometre away, and the watching Wotan men could see the flash of sunlight on glass as the French in the leading half-track had focused their binoculars on the top of the hill. Just behind von Dodenburg and Singh, Schulze whispered to his running mate Matz, 'Watch out, wooden eye, there's trouble brewing.'

'That you can say again,' Matz agreed, as the first half-track started up again, approaching the waiting Germans at a snail's pace. The captured French sergeant tried to say something at the sight. Schulze didn't give him a chance. 'One word from you, old friend,' he threatened, 'and I'll have yer eggs off with a broken bottle.' The prisoner might not have understood the German words, but he'd understood the sweeping gesture Schulze had made at the base of his stomach, as if he were cutting off something very precious to him. He fell silent immediately.

Slowly the half-track came closer and closer. It came to a stop. Nothing moved. But von Dodenburg was well aware that they were being carefully scrutinized by the armed men inside the cab. Finally the steel door swung open and a tall lean French officer, with cropped hair, his shirt starched and pressed immaculately, heavy with three long rows of medal ribbons, stepped out. Carefully and deliberately, the French officer allowed himself to be handed his riding crop and kepi, which he placed on his square head at a jaunty angle in the Gallic fashion.

He came towards von Dodenburg, his pace measured and deliberate. Von Dodenburg thought he knew the type. The

French called them 'burnt heads', professional soldiers, hard-bitten and tough, who had spent their military lives in the colonies, where, in the tribal fighting, no mercy was expected or given.

He stopped in front of the young German officer, eyed him coldly and then swung his right hand up in a long-drawn salute, announcing as he did so, '*Herresbach, Capitaine de l'Infanterie.*'

Von Dodenburg returned the salute in best Wotan fashion, giving his name and saying in French, '*Enchanté, Monsieur le Capitaine.*'

Herresbach cut him short with '*Angenehm, Hauptsturm-führer, wir können Deutsch reden.*'

Von Dodenburg, a north German, didn't recognize the accent. He said, 'You speak German?'

'Yes, I was born German, too. Neuf Brisach in Alsace.' His hard face looked contemptuous. 'But I am not German . . . I am a Frenchman.'*

Instantly von Dodenburg realized the hardbitten French colonial officer didn't like Germans, and at this moment he, von Dodenburg, was going to be the prime object of his dislike.

'I see there has been some trouble,' Herresbach said, pointing his leather riding crop at the dead bodies still littering the hilltop.

For a moment von Dodenburg was at a loss as to what to say. Finally he said, 'Yes, there was a firefight.'

'Between your people and mine, von Dodenburg?'

'Yes,' he admitted reluctantly.

Herresbach looked very serious. 'You realize what this means?' he snapped.

Von Dodenburg felt his temper begin to rise. What right had this officer of a beaten army which had thrown its weapons away the previous year and run for its life before a victorious *Wehrmacht* to talk to him like this? At least the English had continued to fight on after they had fled at Dunkirk. 'No, what does it mean?' he snapped back.

* Most of Alsace-Lorraine was German till the end of World War One.

Von Dodenburg's reaction didn't seem to worry the French officer. He said coldly, 'I shall have to take you into custody, that is what it means, *Hauptsturmführer.*'

Just behind his CO, Schulze growled threateningly and fingered his machine pistol. Von Dodenburg hissed out of the side of his mouth, 'Stand fast, Sergeant!' Then, to Herresbach, 'How can you arrest me? We are not even on French territory. This is not yet French Syria.'

Herresbach reacted immediately. 'I decide what is French territory,' he said, and shrilled a blast on his whistle. As if they had already rehearsed the manoeuvre, the column of half-tracks started up immediately. They split up and came in on either flank of the Wotan men and their prisoners. Von Dodenburg's face fell. He could see that each half-track was packed with infantry, some of them wearing the white kepi of the Foreign Legion; and these were not the pale-faced, bespectacled French conscripts that von Dodenburg had seen throw away their weapons and run for their lives the previous summer. These were hard-faced, bronzed professional soldiers.

'Well?' Herresbach demanded, as his men in their half-tracks came ever closer.

'Well, what?'

'Are you going to surrender?'

'And if I don't?'

'I shall order my men to open fire on you.' He said the words almost carelessly, as if it didn't matter to him one way or the other; as if he was used to killing men without a second thought.

'But you'll kill your own men, our prisoners,' von Dodenburg objected.

Herresbach shrugged. 'Native levies. Riff-raff of no importance.'

Von Dodenburg had known then it was no use. Human life meant little to this hard-faced colonial officer, used to the cruelties of France's colonial wars, and who had probably imbibed his hatred of the *Boche* with his mother's milk back in Alsace-Lorraine. Slowly he had begun to raise his hands. What use would his handful of unarmed soldiers be against Herresbach's troops in their armoured vehicles? It would have been a massacre. Moments later, a bunch of hard-faced legionnaires, all of whom spoke German, were pushing them into the leading half-track, with their corporal saying out of the side of his mouth, *'Arsehole! I hope you frigging well fry in hell, you fascist bastard . . .'*

Over the next few days, stripped naked and existing on water, stale bread and the occasional handful of olives, von Dodenburg had sometimes wished that he was 'frying in hell'. That would, he thought, have been easier than having to undergo the treatment handed out by Herresbach's sadists.

It was clear that Herresbach was playing a double game. While most of the officers of the French Army in Syria were collaborating with their German conquerors, Herresbach, perhaps out of hatred and resentment of the Germans who once ruled his native province, was secretly working against them; perhaps even working for the British, who most Frenchmen thought had betrayed their country by fleeing through Dunkirk in 1940 and leaving her ally in the lurch and at the mercy of the *Boche*.

At all events, Herresbach soon made it clear he wanted information from his prisoner, and that he was prepared to go to any lengths to obtain it. As soon as von Dodenburg had been thrown into the military prison on the charge of having attacked and killed French troops, he had come to see him and made his purpose quite clear. 'Give me what I need to know, German,' he had said, whacking his riding crop against the solitary chair, 'and I shall drop the charge.'

'What do you want to know?' von Dodenburg had asked through swollen lips (for the warders had already given him a good going over with their fists and boots).

'Where is *Obersturmbannführer* Geier and the rest of Battalion Wotan?'

Von Dodenburg was so amazed at the question that he couldn't answer, even if he had known the answer. Surely Herresbach, with what he already knew, should have realized that he and his First Company had been shot down and got separated from the Vulture?

Herresbach had taken his silence for stubbornness. He had signalled the warders and commanded, '*Allez, vite . . .*' Von Dodenburg hadn't heard the rest of his order. For, with a grunted '*sale con*', the bigger of the two warders had punched him in the guts and, before he had time to double up, the second man had kicked him in the testicles. The air had whooshed out of his lungs and he had fallen to the floor, vomit pouring from his gaping mouth.

They hadn't left him there semi-conscious for long. Someone had thrown a pail of cold urine over his face and he had come to, gasping and panting, to be faced by yet another savage beating, which had left him out to the world again.

A day later, Herresbach had come to see him. His face showed no pity when he saw the state von Dodenburg was in – face black-and-blue, lips swollen, eyes virtually hidden in the swellings, his uniform soiled where he had urinated in his pants. Still, if he showed no pity, the tough colonial officer did seem to want to explain himself.

Towering over von Dodenburg, slapping his high polished boot with the swagger stick he always carried as a sign of authority, he said, 'Perhaps you wonder why I need this information from you. What use can it be to a defeated France, whose army wouldn't fight – will not fight. I shall tell you.'

Von Dodenburg wished he had the strength to retort, *I'm not one bit interested in your motives*. But he hadn't. So he listened.

'I hate you Germans, naturally. You are our traditional enemy. I hate the English too. They are an odious treacherous people. At this moment, I am not too happy with my own people, the French. So, why should I bother? The answer is that if we French are ever going to have our national pride once more, we must fight against any enemy that we can imagine. You Germans are our enemy, though we have signed a peace treaty with you. Therefore we must fight you.'

Suddenly von Dodenburg found strength enough to argue,

or perhaps it was just anger at this man, who was, it seemed to him, irrational. 'But how can you fight? To whom would you give this information about us, if I knew it?'

Herresbach didn't appear to listen. His gaze seemed fixed on some distant horizon, known only to him. 'To the Americans,' he answered, in a voice that came from far away.

Despite the weakness of his battered body, von Dodenburg started. 'But the Americans are not even in the war,' he retorted.

Herresbach didn't hear. 'Yes,' he repeated. 'The Americans would welcome that kind of information with open arms – the location of the Führer's favourite SS regiment.' His eyes glittered as he said the words, and it was then that von Dodenburg realized that Herresbach was mad, and that he would never come out of this place alive if he didn't do something about it – soon . . .

Four

The day after Herresbach's strange outburst, they moved von Dodenburg to a larger cell, which even had a thin barred window. Kuno von Dodenburg could find no reason for this move to a cell which actually had several bunks in it, one or two of them with straw mattresses; not particularly clean ones, but a lot softer than the cement slab that he had been chained to down below in the first cell. Not that he tried to. He was content to accept the space and comparative comfort of the larger cell without worrying about it.

That morning, after he had eaten the usual thin soup and hunk of stale black bread the warder shoved through the trap at the base of the cell door, he washed the dirt and caked blood off his sore body the best he could, wiping himself dry with his shirt, the only cloth he possessed, and then took to the cleanest bunk to sleep; he knew that sleep would give him strength and he would need all the strength he could muster if he were to get out of the place alive.

He didn't sleep long, however. Some time in the mid-morning, with the noises of the little frontier town outside penetrating the window of his cell, there was the jingle of keys which signalled the warder's approach, the stamp of heavy boots and drunken curses in German. As weak and exhausted as he was, the fact that whoever was out there was cursing in his native language awoke him at once. He swung his legs off the bunk in the same instant that the door was thrust open by two warders, and a great red-bearded man in the bloodstained white fatigues of the Foreign Legion was flung into the place, crying drunkenly, 'Bunch o' piss pansies. You wait till I get out of here again. I'll make frigging mincemeat o' the pair of you. I swear I will.'

128

'*Merde, assez, sale Boche,*' the bigger of the two warders cursed, and gave the reluctant prisoner a great dig in the small of the back with his club, forcing him back against the wall, glaring at the Frenchmen like a tiger about to spring on its prey while they locked the cell door behind them hastily. Next moment the Legionnaire charged forward as if he were a human battering ram, only to slam head first into the stout oaken door and collapse in a heap on the floor.

Von Dodenburg hobbled stiffly towards the fallen man, held out his hand, saying in German, '*Los, Kamerad, halt fest.*'

The red-bearded giant shook his head like a boxer attempting to avoid a knockout, recognized the uniform and said, 'You're one of them SS fascists, ain't you?' He declined the hand and, with a groan, levered himself up and staggered to the nearest bunk, where he collapsed once more.

Under any other circumstances, von Dodenburg would have been amused by the drunk's reaction. Not now, however. The Legionnaire might be of use to him. He had to cultivate the man, despite his reference to the 'SS fascists'.

'How did you know I was one of the SS fascists?' he asked.

'Yer uniform. I've seen it often enough in the old days,' the drunk said sourly. 'Besides, they put your lot in our barracks. Haven't got a drop of firewater, have you?' He licked his parched cracked lips. 'I could certainly do with sinking a drop behind me collar stud.'

Von Dodenburg shook his head, new energy surging through his battered body. So, Schulze and Matz and the rest of the Wotan-troopers were close at hand. That was a good omen. He hadn't been abandoned altogether. And this drunken giant might be the means of contacting his old comrades in due course. Now he set about establishing a relationship with the man, who obviously was not very keen on his fellow Germans, especially if they were what he called 'fascists', i.e. Nazis.

'Why don't you like fascists?' von Dodenburg persisted, for the drunk seemed calmer now.

The man raised a fist like a small steam shovel. 'Moscow,' he said, as if that were explanation enough.

Von Dodenburg understood. 'You were a member of the old German Communist Party?'

'Yes, Red Front, fought you bastards right to the very end in 1933. Then I did a bunk and ended up in the Legion like a lot of comrades.' He laughed bitterly. 'And look where it got us. We're working for a bunch of French fascists and their German pals.'

Von Dodenburg nodded. 'And you don't like it, eh?'

For the first time, the red-bearded man seemed to take note of his interrogator. He said, 'The Frog fascists have been knocking the German fascist about a bit, ain't they.' He chuckled. 'Makes a nice change.'

Von Dodenburg chuckled too, and, imitating the man's thick Berlin accent, he retorted, 'Can't have liked my big Berlin trap, I suppose.'

'Berliner, eh, just like me. No, we're blessed or cursed with a loose lip in Berlin, I'm afraid. If you've got the wrong party book and a big Berlin trap, you can bet yer life somebody's gonna belt you one.' He slapped his big fist into the palm of his other hand to emphasize his point before drawing out a crumpled pack of cigarettes, saying. 'Fancy a lung torpedo, mate?' The ice had been broken.

Twenty-four hours later, when it came time to release Max, as the Legionnaire was named, von Dodenburg knew he had an understanding with the ex-communist. The latter would find Schulze and the rest of his First Company and tell the big NCO what had happened to their CO. Then von Dodenburg was certain that his old hares would find some way of getting him out of jail before the next bout of torture commenced, as Kuno was certain it would. Yet, at the same time, he was puzzled that Herresbach had had him transferred to the bigger cell, and had even allowed him to have a short-lived cell mate. Was that part of his plan, too? Well, if so, it hadn't worked.

But even as Max prepared to be thrown out to make his own way back to the Legion camp, it appeared he was going to have another cell mate. Down the echoing prison corridor, with the door open for a moment, they could hear Herresbach talking to someone in that unmistakable Alsatian accent of his, though they couldn't identify the language in which the French captain spoke. But there was something about his tone which made von Dodenburg think that he was speaking to someone who was very close to him, though for the life of him, the young officer couldn't imagine anyone who would want to be close to that madman.

Max chanced a peep round the cell door as the heavy stamp of the warders' boots came ever closer. He gave a little gasp and, withdrawing his head, hissed, 'If he comes in here, *Kumpel*, watch yer step.'

'Who?' von Dodenburg asked, noting the urgency in the big ex-communist's voice, but before the latter had time to reply, the first warder was at the door, jingling his keys self-importantly and shouting, '*Allez, vite . . . marche!*'

Max, as tough as ever, raised his big right haunch and ripped off a tremendous fart, saying in German, 'Ride on that one, you frigging asparagus Tarzan.'

Next moment he dodged the blow the warder aimed at him, repeating his warning, 'Watch the little swine. He's frigging trouble on two pretty legs.' And with that he was gone, hurried outside by the impatient warders.

But if Max's exit was rough and brutal, the entrance of von Dodenburg's new cell mate was very gentle indeed, which wasn't surprising. For the newcomer was a mere child, a beautiful one at that.

Von Dodenburg was caught completely by surprise as the boy entered, doffed the cap he was wearing and said in passable French, '*Bonjour M'sieur Le Capitaine. Je m'appelle Ali.*' In a very adult manner, the dark-haired boy with the dark gleaming eyes held out his hand and took von Dodenburg's. His hand was soft and slightly moist, as if he were excited, though for the life of him, von Dodenburg could not see the reason why. All the same, there was something he found distasteful about the beautiful boy, and he withdrew his own hand hurriedly. The boy didn't seem to mind. He sat down without invitation, as the warders closed the cell door behind him gently, and, swinging his bare brown legs, stared at von Dodenburg in silent contemplation, in a manner that made

Kuno feel uneasy. Why, he didn't really know. All he did know was that this kid had been placed in his cell by Herresbach, not by chance, but for a purpose. There was something going on and he had to find out what it was before Schulze started (he hoped) making plans to get him out of the hellhole.

One hour later, unknown to von Dodenburg, of course, Schulze and Matz were already in deep discussion with Max. Although the latter regarded SS officers such as von Dodenburg as fascists, Schulze and Matz were of his own kind, working men who, before Hitler had taken over, might well have voted communist or socialist, but who now, due to circumstances, were members of the National Socialist Party's fighting arm, the *Waffen SS*. Despite their political differences, Max, Matz and especially Schulze, a former 'red' himself, were all working men – 'Frigging cannon-fodder' as the latter put it, 'destined to be sacrificed by the bosses when they think it's necessary.' Naturally Schulze didn't tell Max that he idolized his aristocratic boss, Kuno von Dodenburg.

Now, as they lounged in the Legion's spartan barracks, with the shades drawn to keep the hot afternoon sun out and prevent big ears listening to what they said, Schulze made his approach. 'Comrade,' he said thickly to the ex-communists, for they were already well into a litre bottle of fiery raki which Max had 'organized' – he meant stolen – from somewhere in the great echoing barracks. 'I know your point of view, but you're a German. You can't let one of your own be sacrificed like this by those Frogs. It ain't natural.' He winked at Matz, who was stripped naked on account of the heat and lying on his bunk, occasionally flipping his flaccid penis up and down, as if he were trying to cool himself with it.

'Naturally,' Max agreed. 'But what can we do, comrade? There can't be more than thirty of your lot and, in this battalion, there might be fifty from the homeland who can be trusted. The rest are petty crooks, pimps and pederasts. They'd betray their own mother for a handful of greasy Frog francs.' He spat deliberately on the floor.

'It's enough. We're not going to start a revolution, Max. We just want to get the CO out and then do a bunk.'

'And us? The Frogs'll shoot us out of hand for mutiny if they nab us, Schulzi.'

Schulze laughed easily, as if the future of a bunch of mutinous German-born Legionnaires created no problem. *'Eine Kleinigkeit, alter Freund.* We'll see you fixed up afterwards, especially our CO. As I see it, comrade, you and your lot'll be seeing the rest of this war out lying on some beach, just passing the time of day with as much beer and beaver –' he grabbed the front of his trousers fiercely, as if to make his point quite clear – 'as you can handle. For you, old house, it'll be roses – roses, all the frigging way.'

The red-bearded giant beamed at the thought. 'Great God in Heaven,' he sighed. 'It'll be like Thälmann[*] always promised us, comrade, a Soviet paradise on earth.'

Schulze hadn't the faintest idea what a Soviet paradise on earth was. But he'd agree to anything as long as it freed Kuno von Dodenburg. He slapped Max enthusiastically across the back, so that his false teeth almost popped out of his mouth, and exclaimed, 'Exactly.'

Outside, a miserable Lieutenant Singh, who now found himself, surprisingly, in a Foreign Legion barracks together with a bunch of German communists, wondered what the excitement was within the barracks against which he leaned. Puzzled as he was, however, he was quite sure that Sergeant Schulze and the ugly mug of a red-bearded commie were up to no good. Shaking himself out of his heat-induced reverie, he decided that the matter was worth investigating. Who knew where such an investigation might lead?

[*] Ernst Thälmann, a leading German communist of the '20s and '30s.

BOOK FIVE

End Run At Habbaniyah

One

A corporal cook in a white jacket was lugging a dixie of hot tea across the old parade ground, heading for the bunker which now was his HQ. Jeeves watched, sucking his empty pipe – there had been no tobacco ration for the Habbaniyah garrison for two days now – and the air commodore was suffering just as much as the most humble aircraftsman. Still, there was tea, and Jeeves, the veteran, knew just how much the average British serviceman lived for his 'char'.

Things were bad admittedly. He had already lost half his aircraft, and the men, rationed as they were and working round the clock to defend the base, were exhausted. Still, as long as they got their tea, he knew they'd keep on going; and so far the Iraqis had not mounted that all-out attack that the air commodore had expected ever since Raschid Ali had rebelled against the British.

So, tired as he was, he watched the corporal's progress in a kind of daydream, disregarding the thunder of the Iraqi afternoon barrage. He'd send a couple of his antiquated Gladiator planes against the Iraqi guns as soon as the latter ended their shoot, to try to catch the gunners off guard; it was about all he could do at the moment.

The corporal cook was making heavy going of it as he lugged the big tea urn, and his face was brick-red with the effort. Jeeves knew why: he was worn out like the rest of the garrison. Still the man tried, carrying out his humble duties, as they all were, save the local native levies, who were already beginning to desert in their dozens. But then, that was to be expected. They had little stomach for the fight, especially as

137

they knew that if Raschid Ali succeeded and the British had to abandon Iraq, they'd all be for the chop at the hands of the victors. The mob would rip them to pieces.

Crack! It was like the sound of a dry twig being snapped underfoot on a hot summer's day. The corporal cook stumbled and then sat down abruptly. A red stain had appeared at the breast of his white mess jacket. For what seemed a long time, he simply sat there, still clutching the handle of his bucket. Abruptly he moaned. Next moment he keeled over. The dixie continued to steam next to the dead cook. 'Damnation!' Jeeves cursed, as a heavy machine gun opened up and started spraying the heights from which the sniper had fired and killed the cook. 'The buggers are getting bloody cheeky.'

Next to him the intelligence officer flown in from Baghdad blanched. Like most people in Intelligence, Jeeves thought, he was a 'nervous Nelly'. He'd panicked when he, Jeeves, had suggested that, 'If I could get permission, Captain, I'd bomb Baghdad this very afternoon. Throw every plane I've got into it. Knock the shite out of their ministries. Not exactly Marquis of Queensbury rules – civvies'd get hurt of course – but it's what these Iraqi wags deserve. Treacherous bunch, the whole lot of 'em.' He had puffed vigorously at his empty pipe, while the young Intelligence Corps captain had looked aghast.

'See what I mean, Captain,' Jeeves rubbed it in. 'Can't trust the buggers.' Then he got down to business once more, as the RAF police, all heavily armed, swarmed out across the field looking for more of these hidden enemy killers. 'Fill me in. What do you hear of these Huns who are supposed to be supporting the Iraqi brigade over yonder? My man had no luck in intercepting them.' He meant McLeod, who was out in the desert with his remaining armoured cars once more.

'They reached Baghdad and have been equipped by the Raschid Ali people with civilian lorries and some heavy weapons. We in Intelligence expect them to be leaving the capital for the Iraqi Brigade up in the mountains at any time now. When they arrive, sir, you can expect an immediate attack. From the German wireless intercepts we've picked up from Greece, it appears that the Jerry high command is hopping mad at the delay. They want action here – and they want it soon. And, naturally, this Raschid Ali wallah wants a victory for prestige reasons.'

'I'd give him a bloody victory,' Jeeves grunted darkly, but even as he said the words, he knew that he was hanging on at Habbaniyah by the skin of his teeth. If the combined Iraqis and the trained Huns of the SS did attack together, he'd be surprised if he could hold out more than twenty-four hours. 'All right, Captain, give it to me. When can I expect reinforcements – trained British infantry?'

The young Intelligence captain swallowed hard. 'Not as soon as you'd like, sir.'

'*When?*' Jeeves demanded.

'Well, sir, there's a British infantry battalion from India landing from their troopship at Basra at this moment, sir. Estimating that it'll take them the rest of this day to get ashore with their supplies, then getting the convoy and convoy protection set up—'

'*When?*' Jeeves flashed the young officer a threatening look.

The latter flushed an embarrassed red. 'Sir, my guess is you can't expect reinforcements for another three days, and that—'

'Means –' Jeeves beat him to it – 'the Huns will be here before the brown jobs.'

'Yessir,' the captain answered, looking very crestfallen, as if the delay was his fault.

Jeeves sucked at his pipe like a hungry babe at its mother's nipple. 'Then, Captain, I suggest you go to the armoury and get yourself a Lee Enfield.'

'A Lee Enfield, sir?'

'Yes, a rifle. I'm going to get one too. The way things look, we're going to need everyone who can hold a rifle in the firing line when the balloon goes up.'

Outside, an unshaven, weary-looking aircraftsman was singing tonelessly, '*And the mate at the wheel, had a bloody good feel, at the girl I left behind me.*' Behind him at the Iraqi positions, flares were beginning to sail into the air all along the hill line. Jeeves frowned. At the back of his head, a cynical little voice hissed, 'Soon there's going to be a lot of girls to be left behind.' Then he dismissed the cynical thought from his mind. There was a job to be done and he and his lads were going to do it come what may. 'You,' he snapped at the weary airman. 'Get yourself a shave when the water ration comes up. You're a disgrace to the RAF in that state.'

'Yessir,' the airman said dutifully and without rancour. Air commodore or not, he wasn't going to waste any more precious water shaving. His daily pint of the precious fluid was going to go right down his throat in the form of char when it came up. They were all for the chop one way or another, shaven or unshaven. When the two officers were out of earshot, he resumed singing again about that unfortunate engine driver who disintegrated when his boiler bust, and how the survivors 'found his bollocks, and the same to you . . . Bollocks . . .' It seemed to him to be the most suitable dirge under the circumstances . . .

'Buy,' the old hare growled. 'Buy frigging combs, there's lousy times ahead!'

The Vulture looked hard at the old sweat with the scarred, brutal face, as he joined the other heavily laden troopers climbing aboard the Iraqi trucks. Like most of them, he was drunk, and for once the Vulture didn't object. They had good reason to be drunk. They were disillusioned and depressed, just as he was, in this godforsaken country that lay 'behind the moon', as his troopers swore.

Although they had come so far to help the natives, they had been treated poorly, re-armed with antiquated weapons that dated back to the first war. Even their food was not to soldiers' taste: rice mixed with obscure sauces, and not even a glass of beer to wash the muck down with, due to the locals' religious prejudices. As for women, the ordinary low-ranking stubble-hopper's great compensation, they had turned out to be shapeless creatures, hooded and cloaked from head to foot in black, who hurried away as soon as a soldier looked at them, as if they might be raped the very next instant.

But, for the Vulture, who was interested in neither beer nor women, it was the Iraqi officers who most aroused his ire. They were a pack of scented, fancy-panted idiots, who purported to know their business, but obviously didn't. It was nearly a week now since they had sent up a brigade to attack the RAF base at Habbaniyah. But despite the glowing success reports they had fabricated for the benefit of the rebel politicians under Raschid Ali, that brigade had achieved nothing apart from shelling some of the Tommy positions and killing a few unwary soldiers with their snipers. The Tommies, on the other hand, had inflicted heavy casualties on the natives and their supply columns with their obsolete training planes converted into fighter-bombers.

As far as the Vulture could ascertain, the Iraqi brigade would continue their siege of the Tommies for ever and a day under present circumstances unless, as he had told Dietz, the Wotan adjutant, 'we pull their damned chestnuts out of the fire for them. And you know what that means, Dietz, don't you?'

Glumly the adjutant had nodded his understanding and had said, 'Wotan attacks without Iraqi support and we get a real pasting.'

'Exactly.'

Now, as his troopers prepared to mount up and set off in the convoy bound for the positions of the Iraqi Brigade in the hills to the west of Baghdad, the Vulture's brain raced electrically as he attempted to find some way out of the impasse. For he knew he wasn't going to waste his life here. What he desired from life was more important to him even than those powdered boys with their plucked eyebrows who haunted Berlin's main stations at dusk, delightful as those boyish pavement pounders were. With a longing that was almost sexual, he fervently desired the general's stars that his dead father had once worn. When he had achieved that, he would allow himself to be posted from the SS – he had had enough of being the 'Führer's shitty Fire Brigade'. Wotan's losses were simply too high. He'd aim for a nice safe desk job in the Berlin High Command and let the other fools win the medals and get shot at. There the only action he could anticipate would be in bed with those youthful pavement pounders and their lovely, hairless bodies.

The thought of a job in Berlin as a 'rear-echelon stallion', as they were called contemptuously by the frontline stubble-hoppers, cheered him up for a while, but not for long. For that same old hare standing behind him in the truck who had warned his comrades that it was time to buy combs, for there were 'lousy times ahead' now growled to no one in partic-ular, 'It looks to me, mates, that this one is gonna be a shit or bust op . . . Yes, take my word for it – shit or bust.'

The Vulture opened his mouth to order the big ape to shut up, then thought better of it. The old hare was right again. It was going to be a 'shit or bust' operation. But now he knew, with the one hundred per cent clarity of a sudden vision, that as soon as the 'shitting' started, *Obersturmbannführer* Hans-Egon Geier, known as the Vulture, was going to order 'bust'. His mind was made up. He – Wotan – were going to survive. His mood improved vastly, his gaze no longer taking in the frightening immensity of the barren plain in front of him, he stood erect and, waving his hand above his head, cried, '*Los! Panzer marsch!*'

Slowly, but gathering speed by the instant, the long convoy started to roll forward into the unknown . . .

Two

McLeod was exhausted – and frustrated. It had been seven long days now since Raschid Ali had started his rebellion, and he, personally, felt he had done little to stave off the impending fall of the great Habbaniyah Air Base. Now he knew from British Intelligence, trickling in from their sources still in the capital, that the Germans he had failed to stop a couple of days back were on their way to reinforce the Iraqis besieging the base. Old Iraqi hand that he was, he knew he could run rings around the Germans, who were real greenhorns in the desert. But he knew, too, he had little chance of stopping the advance on Habbaniyah unless a miracle happened. And for the moment, as he peered through his field glasses, he couldn't see any particular miracle on the horizon, just a troop of old-fashioned Iraqi cavalry and an ancient armoured car that had been supplied to the Iraqis by the British authorities. He guessed they were being used as an advance guard on a recce by the Germans.

He lowered his glasses and considered his position. He was in a splendid ambush position, his armoured cars dug in in a hulldown position on a slight rise in a sharp bend on the road from Baghdad. The height and the curve would certainly force any vehicle to slow down to make an ideal target for his gunners. Naturally he had anticipated that the Germans, experts and professionals as they were, would lead with a reconnaissance party, just like the Iraqi one he had just spotted. Under normal circumstances, they would check the road on both sides, especially down below at the ideal ambush spot.

But McLeod thought he had taken care of that eventuality. Half an hour before, a string of camels and mules had passed along the road, goaded up the height by their Iraqi drovers with the normal unthinking cruelty of their kind – they had used sticks with rusty nails in the ends to make the animals keep up the pace. That had caused them to defecate. McLeod had spotted immediately the use to which he could put the still-steaming turds. Once the caravan had passed out of sight, he and his crews had sneaked down to the road and commenced hiding the small Gammon bombs beneath the animal droppings. The Gammons, used as primitive anti-personnel mines, would see off any recce of the general area. He was happy with that.

But he wasn't happy with his own force. Out of the original squadron of a week before – what now seemed another age – he had exactly three 'runners', and one of them was beginning to act up. Three armoured cars, armed with a two-pounder cannon or Vickers machine guns against what Intelligence estimated was a battalion of crack German infantry. If it had been the Iraqis, McLeod knew, a surprise attack, such as he was planning, would have sent the enemy running, pulling off their boots in panic so that they could run faster. But with the Germans, he knew of old from his experiences in the trenches back in 1917, it was different. They might break and run initially. But they'd be back again in double quick time; their professionalism, iron discipline and, he supposed, bravery would see to that. What chance then did his three armoured cars, with limited ammunition, manned by a handful of weary men, stand?

Now, however, McLeod could no longer concern himself with such problems. The enemy reconnaissance party was coming ever closer. Now there was only one problem: should he run or should he stand and fight? For a moment he took his gaze off the advancing enemy and focused a quick glance at his men. They were just ordinary chaps, he knew. They had been dragged from their civilian world of pub, pictures and *palais de danse* and forced to become fighting men. They knew little of empire, save that bit taught them in their council schools, about 'all that red on the map'. What did the King-Emperor and Iraq really mean to them? Children and prod-

144

ucts of the Depression, their main concern had been to find and keep a job in such hard times. Why should they risk their lives for a concept that meant little to them? Why die now for this arsehole of the world when the Labour politicos were telling them that after the war they would participate in a 'brave new world'? He was a regular, a 'lifer' as the conscripts called his type. He was paid to die. Should he sacrifice their lives? For what?

'Here the wogs come.' 'Porky' Peters, the fattest man in the squadron, broke into his urgent reverie. 'Served up on a silver platter, like, sir. Cor, fuck a duck, they won't know what hit 'em, sir, will they?'

'No, they won't,' he heard himself replying with new enthusiasm. His mind was made up. 'All right, lads, stand by yer guns.'

Now the reconnaissance party was spreading out to both sides of the road, with the armoured car itself on the dusty white road, its turret moving slowly from side to side like the snout of some primeval monster scenting out its prey. The cavalry had drawn their swords and the watching men could see the sun gleam off the curved sabres. But the Iraqis didn't look one bit martial, despite the drawn sabres. Indeed, McLeod could almost sense their fear as they approached the curve in the hill road, as if they already suspected that trouble lay behind it somewhere. 'Wait till yer see the whites of their eyes,' he joked quietly in order to relieve the tension.

'I'll be happier, sir,' Porky whispered back, 'when I see the whites of their arses when they do a bunk.'

The others laughed and McLeod felt ever more confident; the men were bearing up well.

Five minutes passed on leaden feet. The cavalry were spreading out even more, the riders stopping their mounts every now and again to search the horizon, or bending over their saddles to check the ground below. McLeod prayed they didn't suspect that there might be mines there. That would be fatal to his daring, almost suicidal, plan.

Meanwhile the little enemy armoured car was slowing down as it rumbled into the curve at the pass. Behind McLeod, the

145

armoured car armed with the two-pounder cannon – not very powerful, but with enough punch, McLeod believed, to penetrate the Iraqi's armour – swung the gun round and started to focus on the Iraqi vehicle, which was now doing less than ten miles an hour.

Tension mounted. McLeod could sense a nerve ticking at his temple, and his shirt was wet with sweat and clinging to his back unpleasantly: all signs of high tension. He ignored them and concentrated on what was to come, knowing that the one to strike the first punch might well be the winner.

The gunner peered through his sight. He tried to ignore the beads of sweat dripping from his forehead and threatening to blind him. Slowly, with an air of finality, the armoured car, moving at a snail's pace, now crept into the circle of calibrated glass. Gently, very gently, the gunner's hand, again damp with sweat, fell down and found the firing lever. He clenched his wet fist around it. The enemy armoured car was now almost stationary as its obviously fearful commander took it round the end of the curve, wondering probably what awaited him there.

McLeod wet his lips, which were suddenly very parched. 'Ready, gunner?' he asked in a husky voice. God how he wished the nerve would cease ticking!

'Ready, sir.'

'Range two hundred.'

'Two hundred, sir.' The gunner adjusted his sight slightly. He could see every detail of the enemy car now – the rusty rivets, the oil trace leaks, the fresh wet marks where someone had pissed against its bullet-proof tyre.

McLeod counted to three. Suddenly he felt a great burst of energy surge through his emaciated skinny frame. '*Fire!*' he yelled with all his strength.

The almost unbearable tension relieved at last, the gunner pulled the firing lever. A boom. The sharp crack of the armour-piercing shell leaving the two-pounder. The armoured car reared back on its back axle, like a wild horse being put to the saddle for the first time. To its front, the sand twirled up in a sudden yellow cloud. Next instant there was the white blur of an armour-piercing shell zipping flatly across the inter-vening distance at the Iraqi vehicle.

At that range, the gunner couldn't miss. There was the hollow boom of steel striking steel. The enemy vehicle shook violently, as if struck by a gigantic fist. For a moment nothing seemed to happen. Then, suddenly, startlingly, it sagged. Both rear tyres burst. It sank to the ground. An instant later a black mushroom of smoke started to rise from its open turret.

The cavalry scattered at once. Slashing their whips and reins against the sweat-gleaming flanks of their mounts, they spread to left and right, crouching low in their saddles in the same instant that the other two gunners opened up with their Vickers machine guns. In a lethal white noise, five hundred bullets a minute zipped towards the riders. Here and there men were ripped from their saddles. Riderless horses, some dragging their masters behind them by the stirrup, ran crazily across the desert in an attempt to escape that deadly white killer. Not for long. Almost immediately they ran into the turds hiding the anti-personnel mines.

What happened now wasn't war – it was a cruel heartless massacre. Horses flew through the air. Great haunches of horseflesh littered the desert in a disgusting blood-red chaos. Others were down on their forelegs, eyes wild with fear, strug-gling to rise and get away from this place of sudden, violent death. To no avail. They moved and hit another mine, shat-tering their bodies so that in some cases the gleaming white ribcages were revealed, glittering like polished ivory against the setting of that blood-red gore.

Their riders fared no better. They swung themselves off their mounts in their panic, or tried to control the crazy bleeding steeds, which danced on their hind legs, pawing the air in crazy fury with their forelegs. But the riders didn't get far. Trying to dodge the death-bringing little brown pats of faeces, they invariably stepped or slipped into another and were abruptly reduced to the size of dwarves, standing somewhat ludicrously, bewildered momentarily, before they overbal-anced and fell forward on their bleeding shattered stumps, dead before they hit the ground . . .

The Vulture realized immediately what had happened. He could not see what was happening beyond the curve, but he guessed. The damned fool native reconnaissance party had run straight into an ambush or something of that kind and, by the sound of the screams and the agonizing cries coming from round the bend, they were getting the worst of it. He didn't hesitate. Trained professional that he was, with nearly two years of combat behind him, he cried to a startled, white-faced Dietz. 'De-bus. You take right flank . . . I'll take the left . . . At the double now . . . *Schnell . . . dalli, dalli, Leute!*'

His old hares reacted at once. '*Los!*' they cried to the greenhorns. 'Come on, you greenbeaks. Out . . . *Los, Menschenskinder!* Do you want to live for ever, you dogs!'

Within the minute, the soldiers were dropping from their trucks and forming up into skirmish lines on both sides of the stalled convoy, with both Dietz and the Vulture leading from the front, as good SS officers should.

The panzer grenadiers, for most of the Vulture's remaining men were grenadiers – armoured infantry – lacked the cover of the tanks with which they usually worked. Still they kept their old formations, avoiding the inexperienced soldier's tendency to group together and make a better target for enemy fire in extended orders, with NCOs to left and right flank and their officers out front setting an example. They advanced to the tiny British position on the hillside beyond the cover, as confident as ever that no one could withstand the SS, especially SS Wotan, the elite of the elite. They came on slowly, bodies slightly bent, as if fighting a strong wind, weapons held at the high point across their young bodies, eyes fixed firmly on their front. But even the old hares among them were tense, their bodies held rigid, awaiting that first chatter of death and the hard steel striking their soft flesh.

None came. Squadron Leader McLeod was just as much a veteran as were the old hares. He knew his men were scared. Who wouldn't be, facing the advance of several hundred armed Germans with only a handful of men? They'd tend to open fire before the Germans got within the killing ground, if he didn't watch them; and he couldn't allow that. Every round now counted; every round would have to find a target. 'Steady on, lads,' he urged in a low voice. 'Stand fast, we've got the buggers by the short and curlies. Steady.' Whether his words encouraged his men, McLeod didn't know. But while they fiddled with the bolts of their rifles, as nervous soldiers did, they didn't open fire. Only the gunner in the lead armoured car moved, switching his turret from side to side, as if impatient to begin the killing.

McLeod frowned. He'd kill a great many of the Germans if he could catch them at short range. But what if the SS didn't panic, break and retreat? What then? They'd swamp his positions and that would be that. Now was the time, if he was to save his little command, to give the Germans a short sharp shock and then run like hell.

He shook his head. He knew he couldn't do that. If the Germans didn't break and run under that first volley of withering fire, he knew in his heart of hearts he wouldn't run for it; he'd fight to the end.

Now all was silent save the squeak of the armoured-car turret being swung to left and right, the heavy breathing of the waiting men and the slither of the Germans advancing stolidly, purposefully, like a line of automatons, through the sand.

'*Two hundred yards* . . .' McLeod started to count off the distance between his own position and the German line, squinting against the sun, the sweat streaming down his brick-red face. '*One hundred and seventy* . . .' Now he could see the strained individual faces beneath the coal-scuttle helmets. They were kids really, he told himself, but vicious hard-boiled kids with murder in their hearts. '*One hundred and fifty yards* . . .' That was far enough.

He raised himself above cover and in a voice that surprised him because of its vigour and strength, cried, 'Fire, lads . . . *Fire at will!*'

They needed no urging. The tension snapped at last. The little position erupted in a burst of vicious fire. The slaughter had commenced.

Three

'F art cannon!' Schulze sneered, as *Capitaine* Herresbach strode across the baked white parade ground of the Legion's barracks, slapping his swagger stick against the side of his highly polished riding boot.

Max, as tough as he was, looked worried. 'Watch it, Schulzi, you big ox, you don't play games with that Alsatian bugger. He can sniff out yer thoughts even before yer can think them.'

Schulze pulled a face. 'He can sniff up my hairy ass, as far as I'm concerned.' Then he dismissed the tough French officer. 'What's the score?' he asked.

'They're with us, even the two Yids. They've had enough of the Legion and Captain Herresbach.'

Schulze guffawed and gave Matz a tremendous dig which nearly sent the smaller man flying. 'Did you hear, you perverted banana-sucker. We're gonna have German Yids on our side. Think o' that. Yids as honorary members of the SS.'

Matz was not impressed. 'You're gonna be minus one genuine German SS man, comrade, if you keep knocking him about like that. You don't know yer own frigging strength.' He rubbed his bruised ribs, counting them to see if they were all intact.

Schulze ignored the comment, as the three continued walking and plotting in the afternoon shade of the Legion barracks. 'That means we've got about fifty effectives,' he said. 'That should be enough to tackle the lock-up and get the CO out.'

'*Einverstanden*,' the red-bearded Legionnaire agreed. 'But the problem is what are we gonna do next after we've got your officer out? Herresbach'll rouse the whole garrison, knowing him. Then the question is where do we go? Deeper into Syria?'

Schulze pondered the questions for some moments, while Matz picked his nose, listening to the wail of the Mullah calling the faithful to prayers in the village. 'What about back to Iraq?' he suggested. 'After all, the dump is supposed to be on our side.'

Schulze scratched his shaven head. 'All this thinking isn't good for me,' he complained. 'Thinking should be left to officers and gents. They get paid to do it.'

'Well, we ain't got no officers and gents,' Matz said firmly. 'So we've got to think this out now by ourselves. The CO probably won't like it, but I say we should go back to Iraq. Perhaps we can contact our own people there, and they'll get us away from this dump. I've had enough of the exotic east to last me a lifetime. Besides, Herresbach perhaps won't be expecting to go east instead of west. After all, we were running away to Syria when that arse with ears nabbed us.'

Max looked from the one to the other, knowing that his own fate was linked to their decision. He knew he didn't want to stay in Syria much longer, but at the same time he didn't want these SS types to talk him into going back to the Fatherland. It'd be good to see his old dad again after so many years in exile. But the Gestapo'd soon have him back behind the Swedish curtains* again, and this time he'd not come out. He said, as the two others still had not made up their minds, 'Well, come on you two, piss or get off the pot!'

'All right, once we get the CO out, we head into Syria. That's it. Now, how do we go about getting him out? I mean,' he added swiftly, 'we can't trust any of the other rabble here in the barracks, and there'll be fifty of us leaving the dump, all armed. It's bound to be noticed.'

'Not tomorrow at dawn,' Max cut in swiftly. 'Number One Company is off on a punishment march. Thirty kilometres in full field marching order, with their packs filled with rocks. It's Herresbach's orders. He didn't like their turnout the other morning.'

* Slang for prison bars.

'But how can that be cover for us, Max?' Matz asked.

'We join 'em. I'll bribe the sergeant-major. We'll bring up the rear. As soon as we're in the town, we do a bunk.'

'But can you trust the sergeant-major?' Schulze queried. 'There'll be questions asked afterwards and Herresbach is no dummy. He hasn't fallen on his mouth. If he finds out about the sergeant-major—'

Max held up his big dirty hand for silence. 'He's got the hots for the Druse girl in the Legion's bar downtown. The one with the tits like silken pillows. I swear I'd give my own left ball to get my piece of salami up her knickers. Well, all he needs is this.' He made the continental gesture of counting money with his finger and thumb. 'Once she sees that, it'll be an instant love-match and she'll have her drawers down in zero comma nothing seconds. The lucky bastard.' He licked his abruptly dry lips.

'I know the feeling,' Schulze said. 'If this goes on, I'll be impotent before the frigging week's out.'

'Get on with it,' Matz urged. 'Looks as if we've got visitors.' He jerked his head to the right.

The other two stared for a moment. It was Lieutenant Singh on one of his usual walks around the barracks, for Herresbach had been uncertain what to do with this strange educated Indian in the uniform of a German officer. In the end, he had paroled him to the barracks and one kilometre around the place. So it was that, apart from taking his meals at the barracks – and even then he was not admitted to the French officers' mess – he was on his own with no duties to carry out save to prowl around the camp, eyes everywhere, as if he were looking for something specific, though Matz and Shulze, who disliked the Indian officer, could not fathom what it was. All the same, the two old comrades were certain Singh was up to no good, and tended to avoid him whenever they could.

Matz nudged the big sergeant. 'Come on, Schulzi – and you too, Max, let's go to the canteen. You can buy us a rouge, Max.'

Max made a rude gesture with a middle finger that looked like a fat hairy pork sausage. Matz ignored it and together the three of them headed for the wet canteen, deep in conversation, watched by a Lieutenant Singh who was stroking his chin thoughtfully . . .

It seemed to a bored, impatient von Dodenburg that the handsome boy had been watching him day and night without respite. All he appeared to do was to sit on the edge of his bunk, swinging his legs back and forth, occasionally sucking his thumb like a much smaller child (though he did it in a way that von Dodenburg couldn't help thinking was sexually provocative), and staring at him with an inane smile on his pretty face. Why? Kuno asked himself time and time again – and to what purpose had this kid, who didn't speak a word of German and only poor French, been placed in a cell with an adult like himself? There were many questions and few answers.

The one thing that Kuno von Dodenburg *was* certain about was that the boy was a creature of *Capitaine* Herresbach. At regular intervals during the day, the Alsatian officer, bearing gifts for the boy, came bustling in, all smiles, his usual hard face benign and, Kuno couldn't help thinking, almost loving. For a few moments the two of them would chat animatedly together in one of the native languages of Syria, and Kuno could have sworn that, if he hadn't been there, Herresbach would have kissed the boy when their heads were together whispering some secret or other.

For a while Kuno dismissed the boy and concentrated on his own problem. It was clear to him that Herresbach had taken the law into his own hands, which he could, being the virtual master of this remote border outpost. His fate, and the fate of his men, lay in the Alsatian's hands. But Herresbach couldn't seem to understand that he, Kuno, had lost all contact with the Vulture and the rest of SS Assault Battalion Wotan. What could he know about the battalion's present position? All the same, Herresbach was going to keep him imprisoned like this, and his men in a kind of open arrest in the Legion's barracks until he revealed the information that he didn't have.

Now everything, therefore, depended upon Schulze and the old hares of Wotan. He knew by now that Schulze was going to attempt to rescue him from the prison, and it wouldn't be too difficult, providing his men were well armed. The warders, mostly middle-aged Frenchmen serving out their time until they received their pension, were no match for his SS troopers. But, as with every solution, there was a new problem. What was he going to do when his men did rescue him? He had no desire to go back to Iraq. For him that country was finished; it was not worth the life of a single Wotan trooper. Yet undoubtedly Herresbach would alert the whole of the Iraq-Syrian border area once they had escaped – and, he guessed, the French authorities wouldn't take too kindly to Germans escaping from one of their prisons, especially if French were killed or injured in the breakout.

'*Tu?*' The boy's oddly feminine voice broke into his reverie. He looked up sharply. '*Tu veux?*' The boy was holding his limp little penis in his hand suggestively.

Von Dodenburg blushed in spite of himself. He had seen a lot of things in these years of war since 1939, but nothing as disgustingly provocative as this pretty boy offering his body so unashamedly.

The boy jerked his flaccid organ up and down, smiling winningly all the time, mouth slightly open, licking his wet, red lips with his cunning little pink tongue. It was too much for Kuno. 'Why, you little swine!' he gasped. Without thinking of the consequences, he stepped forward and slapped the boy so hard that his head jerked to one side, his face flushing an immediate deep red where he had been slapped. Next moment he started to wail, tears of pain running down his cheeks.

Kuno von Dodenburg towered above the weeping boy, fists clenched, as if he were restraining himself by a sheer effort of will power from striking the perverted child once again.

But that wasn't to be. The boy's cry of pain had alerted someone further down the prison passage. There was the sound of heavy boots running along the flags. A jingle of keys. The heavy door was flung open with a rusty creak. Next instant half a dozen warders fell on Kuno von Dodenburg and started beating him with boot and fist. He fell to the floor, curled up like a ball. To no avail. A boot thudded into his groin. He yelled in agony, a yell that was cut when the vomit filled his mouth. A moment later another boot slammed into the side of his head and he blacked out.

He came to, crumpled in the foetal position on the floor, his head in a mess of his own vomit. The cell was silent now. The warders who had assailed him had gone back to the daily routine of smoking and playing cards and the odd swig at their bottles of raki. For that he was grateful; he wanted time to recover.

Still, the rage that burned within him made him forget his aches and pains; and it was a rage that was inspired not only by the cruel treatment he had just received, but also by the mission and these countries in which that mission was to be carried out. They were, it seemed to him, infinitely corrupt and decadent. They were not worth conquering or liberating, whichever way one looked at it. The sooner he and his men were out of them the better.

For he knew his torturers would be back. Herresbach's tame little male whore had failed to seduce him into talking; now they would use strong-arm treatment on him, and he had no illusions about his ability to withstand long-time torture.

Now, as he forgot the pain and tried to repress his forebodings about what his captors might do to him – and, after the handsome boy prostitute, he felt they'd use sexual means of some kind to extract the information they felt he knew – he tried too to visualize how Schulze and the rest would attempt to free him.

He knew that Schulze, like he would himself, would try to avoid casualties. Over the years, he had attempted to knock that precept into the minds of his company at all levels. *Train hard, fight easy* had been his motto. So how would they attempt to free him without too many casualties? Was there some way for them to get within the prison without a fight, and then deal with the handful – probably – of warders on duty? That would mean, he told himself, that their best time for the rescue attempt would be at night, when the number of people on duty would be lower. Would they use a bluff to get inside the prison? If they had recruited some of Max's Legionnaires to help them, they might well be able to do so; for Max and his fellow Legionnaires spoke French as well as their native German. What then?

But, try as he might, von Dodenburg could not make his tired mind go any further. It simply refused to work on the problem any more. So, lying there on the hard concrete floor, his nostrils assailed by the stink of his own vomit, Kuno began to drift off into an uneasy sleep.

He awoke with a start, wondering where he was, and then, when he realized he was in his cell, what had awakened him. A moment later another burst of the drunken familiar chorus told him more than what had startled him out of his sleep. It was that old Swabian ditty, sung in dialect, which military bands always played when soldiers left a garrison. How often had he warbled it himself over these last years, standing on some chill lonely station at midnight or marching through the cheering streets with the kids waving flags and the excited womenfolk pelting the grinning singing troops with flowers.

It was '*Muss i denn, muss i denn . . . zum Städele hinaus.*' But there was something strange about this rendition of the sentimental Swabian song. After each chorus, a collection of bass voices yelled 'Boom . . . boom . . . boom!' They did it several times, and each time the 'booms' came in threes, until finally they disappeared into the distance, heading probably for the Legion's barracks, and the song died away with them.

Suddenly he had it. He sat up with a start. 'Must I leave the town?', were the words of the ditty. Who? He, Kuno von Dodenburg, of course. And the '*boom . . . boom . . . boom*', always three times. His battered face lit up. Of course, Schulze and his pals were coming to get him out at three this very morning. If he had been a praying man, the arrogant young SS officer would have been on his knees praying that moment. But he had long given up religion in favour of the new one taught by the God of the SS, Adolf Hitler. So, instead he contented himself with preparing for the escape to come.

Four

There were three of them left now. The rest were dead, spread out in the desert at extravagant angles like thrown-away broken dolls. All the armoured cars had been hit and there was no chance of escape with the vehicles. Still they fought on, encouraged by McLeod, his arm hanging shattered at his side, the blood streaming down from it in torrents.

By now the Germans had them surrounded. Yet they seemed scared to press home their final attack, on account of the armoured car armed with the two-pounder cannon. They didn't know, of course, that McLeod and his two companions had only armour-piercing shells left; not of much use against infantry.

Still McLeod, feeling, at times, he might faint at any moment due to the loss of blood, was grateful for the 'pea-shooter', as they had called the ineffectual weapon contemptuously. It gave them time to try to raise the base and give the location of the Germans. Perhaps Jeeves might be able to spare one of his obsolete planes to attack them, though McLeod doubted it. He knew just how short both pilots and petrol were at the Habbaniyah Base. Still, he could try.

Now, as the sweating radio operator with the bloodstained bandage wrapped round his head tried to raise Habbaniyah, McLeod waited for the Germans to attack again. He knew they would. The Germans never gave up; they were almost as fanatical as the Japs. That's why they had to be defeated. If Iraq fell into their hands, Persia would follow, and eventually the whole of the Muslim Middle East. If the Japs attacked in the East, as everyone expected them to do sooner or later, and started to march westwards, India would go over to them,

157

they'd link up with the Germans in the Middle East, and that would mean the end of the British Empire. Not that he was a one hundred per cent advocate of the Empire – it had its defects. But it was a damned sight better and cleaner than the Jap and Jerry empires, or any other one that would follow it.

'Sir.' It was the gunner manning the two-pounder who broke urgently into his reverie. 'Here the friggers come again, sir.' He pressed the trigger of the co-axial Vickers machine gun and sent a burst of tracer winging in the direction of the SS, who had risen from their positions to the left and were stumbling forward in a kind of awkward run in the deep sand.

Abruptly the front rank of the slow figures was galvanized into violent action. They danced, waved their hands and were bowled over, howling with pain, like a bunch of puppets at the hands of a puppet master who had suddenly gone crazy. Still the next rank came on, stumbling and falling over the writhing bodies of their dying comrades, advancing with deadly purpose, and McLeod knew they'd keep coming like this until they killed their enemies or were killed themselves. This was the last German assault. 'Use the popgun – anything. Radio operator, man your weapon.' He picked up the tommy gun he had chosen for himself and, standing upright in the turret of the damaged armoured car, loosed off a violent blast.

'Tommies!' Dietz gasped, as the firing erupted once again and his grenadiers began falling all around him. 'Don't the tea-drinking swine know when to give up, blast their eyes!'

It was obvious to him and the Vulture, ready to lead the second stage of the final attack on the other flank, that they didn't. They'd stand and fight to the bitter end, and the Vulture knew he couldn't waste too many men on this handful of stubborn Tommies. The Führer would never forgive him if he allowed his 'fire brigade', SS Assault Battalion Wotan, to be wiped out in this godforsaken place to no real purpose.

He cursed as yet another half a dozen of Dietz's grenadiers went down under the fire from the embattled little position on the top of the hill. This couldn't go on, he cursed again. He had to do something, something drastic to finish off the buck-teethed Tommies once and for all.

Then he had it. He'd burn the swine out.

McLeod felt very weak now. His vision was blurred and he felt he might faint from loss of blood at any moment. He could see that his two companions were in no better shape. They had both been wounded once more in the last German attack, and the sergeant who had manned the Vickers had been particularly badly hit. The end of his long nose was white and pinched, a sure sign that he didn't have long to live. Still he stuck to his post. They'd die here, he told himself, but they'd make the Germans pay the price.

For a moment or two, as the small-arms battle gave way to desultory German sniper fire, his mind wandered and he remembered how it had been when he had first come out to Iraq straight from the trenches in France. It had been a revelation to get away from the mass slaughter of trench warfare, the eternal Northern French fog and drizzle, to this country of the glaring sun and the breathtaking heat.

In those days, they had all been a little like the legendary Lawrence of Arabia. He had been their hero and they had aped him in dress and habits. They had worn Arabic togs and eaten Arabic food, including sheep's eyes swallowed whole. Most of them had learned Arabic too, and had been advocates of the nomadic Arab way of life, aware of the distinction between them and the city dwellers who had tamely accepted the Turkish yoke and had been unprepared to fight for their freedom as the Arabs under Lawrence had done.

He – they – had been wrong of course. The Arabs, 'the sons of the desert', as the cheaper British newspapers had called them, had been just as vile and venal as their former Turkish masters. Lawrence, a terrible pervert, as they had discovered much later, had led him and all those keen, clean-living young Englishmen of that time astray. For nearly a decade the English Arabists and their diplomatic masters at the Foreign Office, who had subscribed wholeheartedly to the Arab cause, too, had been fooled into supporting the 'sons of the desert'. They had allowed them to build up their little kingdoms and principalities, while the oil discovered all the time in their remote desert wastes had become ever more important. Then these nomads, who, back in the early '20s, had been penniless illiterates living in their black tents, surrounded by a bunch of half-starved dependents they called their tribe, had begun to show their true selves. With British help they had gotten rid of the Turks. Now they wanted to rid themselves of the British, too, and they had been prepared to use any means to do so. Finally they had turned to the sworn enemies of the British Empire, Italy and Germany, and the same people who had sworn eternal friendship to those young idealistic British officers so long before, would now gladly stab them in the back if they could.

McLeod sighed. What a waste it had all been! What a waste, in reality, his own life had been too, year after year out here under the searing sun, which had burned the very sap out of him and had turned him into the ageing, embittered man he had become: a man without family, without a future, without interests, save these same hawk-nosed people whom he now detested. He sighed again. Perhaps it would be better if it ended here in battle. At least he'd go down fighting, instead of becoming some crusty old fogey, retired to Cheltenham, who wrote angry letters to *The Times* on subjects which interested no one.

'Sir.' It was his sergeant.

'Yes?'

'They're coming again, sir. Near that bunch of camel thorn at three o'clock, sir.'

Wearily, as if his head was worked by rusty springs, McLeod turned his head to the right and looked in the direction indicated by the NCO.

A couple of riflemen were advancing warily towards them, rifles at the ready, with, between them, another German, unarmed, it seemed, with his shoulders bent almost as if he were a hunchback.

Suddenly McLeod had it, though his brain was too exhausted for him to take in the full import of what he had just recognized: something he had not seen since it had frightened the living daylights out of him at the Third Battle of Ypres, back in '17. 'Oh my God!' The exclamation came tumbling out of his abruptly gaping mouth involuntarily.

'What is it, sir?' the sergeant asked, busy tapping the anti-quated Vickers machine gun round so that he could focus on the strange little party advancing upon them warily, obviously ready to hit the sand if they came under direct fire before they reached 'the dead ground', some fifty metres from the stalled armoured car.

McLeod could hardly bring himself to say the word, but he knew he had to. 'Flame thrower!'

The sergeant took his hands away from the Vickers, shocked beyond belief, his sunburnt face abruptly ashen. 'Holy Christ! A flame thrower, sir!'

McLeod wasted no more time; he knew he had none to waste. Once the flame-thrower party reached the dead ground, the three defenders would be finished. He jerked up his tommy gun and pressed the trigger hard. Nothing!

He pressed the trigger again. Once more there was no response. The sub-machine gun lay impotent and silent in his hands. He had a stoppage.

Somehow the three Germans seemed to guess the defenders were in trouble. By now the Englishmen should have been firing at them. They wasted no time. '*Alles für Deutschland!*' Wildly they yelled the battle cry of the Armed SS, rushing forward, the deadly pack bouncing up and down on the back of the man in the middle. '*Tod den Tommies!*'

Crazily McLeod cried to the operator with the bloodstained bandage around his head. 'Knock out the man in the middle . . . For God's sake!'

The operator fired. And again. Both his slugs missed, digging up spurts of sand at the SS men's flying feet. McLeod slammed the butt of his tommy gun against the turret of the armoured car in one last desperate burst of rage and frustra-tion. He fired the next instant. The stoppage was cleared. The weapon was working. Too late!

Gasping like ancient asthmatics in the throes of some final attack, the three Germans flung themselves full length into the dead ground. McLeod tensed for what was to come.

He didn't have to wait long. There was a sinister hiss. It was like some primeval monster emerging from the slime to utter its first fiery fetid breath. The very air seemed to tremble. A crack like a rod being struck against a hollow piece of metal. Next moment a blue, oil-tinged bar of flame swept out from the dead ground, seeking its prey.

McLeod felt the air being drawn from his lungs by that terrible, all consuming heat. Frantically he choked for breath. To his front the sand blackened at a tremendous rate as the spurt of flame ran towards them. It engulfed the front of the armoured car. The paintwork immediately spat and bubbled like the symptoms of some loathsome skin disease. McLeod dropped the useless gun; he'd need it no more. Next moment the flame had surrounded him, blinding him at once, the greedy little red fingers tearing at his flesh, blackening it and splitting it, the flesh beneath a cooked pink, and then it was all over and he was dead, and the Vulture was yelling his new order above the crackle of the dying flames. 'We march west . . . SS Assault Battalion Wotan – *move out!*'

Jeeves was sitting in the sandbagged bar of the officers' mess, morosely contemplating the quarter of a bottle of Haig, when the news came. Outside, the Iraqi artillery was laying on a tremendous barrage and, with the enemy SS battalion on its way, he guessed that the last attack on Habbaniyah Base would commence within the next few hours – and that would be that. 'Don't be vague, order Haig.' He repeated the sales jingle of the whisky company, wondering if this last bottle would hold out to the end of the great siege. He wouldn't like to fall into Iraqi hands sober. 'That would be very unwise – remember Kut[*],' he said, half aloud, in the fashion of nearly drunk men who are beginning to wax philosophical.

It had been about then that young Adrian Smythe-Jones had strode into the bar, full of good cheer, his slightly weak face beaming. 'Good news, sir!' he cried across the room,

[*] After the British garrison surrendered the fortress of Kut to the Turks in WWI, the garrison suffered terrible atrocities at the hands of their captors, including those who would be regarded today as Iraqis.

which in a proper pre-war regular RAF mess was not the done thing.

Jeeves frowned. He didn't like the pilot, with his 'Pilot Officer Prune' handlebar moustache and the top button of his tunic undone as if he were a survivor of the Battle of Britain, one of the bloody 'few', which he patently wasn't – he was still in training. Now, however, he forgot his dislike as he spun round and snapped, 'What do you mean – good news? There's no bloody good news left in this bloody world, young man.'

The young pilot wasn't put out. 'But there is, sir,' he persisted. 'Fifteen minutes ago, I buzzed the Hun column. The old kite wasn't up to bombing. She'd gone and got a poxed-up bomb—'

'For God's sake, get on with it!' Jeeves interrupted him angrily.

'Well, sir. They're off.'

'Off where?'

'Heading west, well away from the base. To my way of thinking, they're on a westerly course for the Syrian frontier. Do you think I could have a beer, sir? My mouth's like a monkey's armpit.'

'Have a bloody barrel, if there's that much left in the mess!' Jeeves cried exuberantly, for, as if to confirm the young pilot's information, the intense Iraqi artillery barrage had ceased with startling suddenness, leaving behind it a loud echoing silence.

It was only later, when the great news was spreading through the mess, and outside to the exhausted 'erks' who had been getting ready for the final battle, that Air Commodore Jeeves reminded himself to ask, 'Any sign of Squadron Leader McLeod, Smythe-Jones?'

The young pilot raised his head from his pint glass, the foam dripping from his absurd moustache. 'Not a sausage, sir,' he answered a little thickly. 'But I suppose he'll turn up sooner or later. You know these old Iraqi hands. They always come up smelling of roses, sir.'

'Yes, I suppose you're right, young man,' Jeeves agreed reluctantly. 'Smelling of roses . . . what . . .'

BOOK SIX

Defeat and Victory

One

'*P*<i>as bon</i>,' the whore whispered, as Schulze shoved her against the wall. The gendarme patrol had just gone past and, seeing the big Legion soldier fumbling with the cheap tart against the wall of the prison, the cops had laughed, made a few obscene suggestions, and had gone on their way, certain that nothing suspicious was going on here. Now Schulze thought he might as well enjoy the whore before the fireworks started.

'Why *pas bon*?' he whispered hoarsely, proud of the newly learned French, but still eager to get at it 'like a fiddler's elbow' as well.

'You too big. Me too small,' she answered. 'I not accommodate you, *chéri*.'

'Don't worry. I'll look after yer cherry,' Schulze answered confidently. 'Turn round.' He grabbed the little tart by the hips, turned her round and flung up her skirt to reveal her plump naked buttocks. He slapped them lightly.

She giggled softly and whispered. 'You naughty soldier.'

'I'm gonna be naughtier,' Schulze said, fumbling for his flies, 'before long. Now hold still and prepare to take a chunk of honest German salami on board.' She giggled again, as something hard and impatient started to press against her soft bottom.

Preoccupied as he was, Schulze could hear the soft noises at the end of the street all the same. It was his comrades, their spare pair of socks pulled over their boots to muffle the noise. It would be starting soon, but he was determined to get a little bit of the other before it did. As he had confessed to his running mate Corporal Matz before he had left the barracks with the whore who Max had found for him, 'She'll stand on her head naked on the *Rue Principale* for a handful of francs and something to sniff up her hooter,' he'd said – 'Yer never know, old house. I don't want to die a virgin.'

He found it. He grunted and pushed harder. She giggled yet again and wriggled her buttocks like a teenager experiencing her first sex. 'Old bag,' Schulze muttered in his usual gentlemanly fashion, 'keep frigging still till I get it all—'

It was at that very moment that a heavy weight landed on his broad back. Strong as an ox as Schulze was, he was caught by surprise and was thrust forward rudely. '*Attention!*' the whore cried in alarm as his organ thrust deep inside her. 'My eyes, they pop!'

They popped again a second later as someone else landed on Schulze's back and followed Matz as he scrambled up the rough wall, heading for the roof of the prison. For the next few seconds, Schulze withstood the weight of several Legionnaires and Wotan troopers, as they used him as a kind of a bridge to assist them scale the wall. Finally he gave up, as the whore's knees gave way and she slumped to the cobbles, crying, 'Oh la, la. You Boche, what a salami!'

For a moment Schulze was undecided whether he should be angry or complimented by her remark. In the end, as Max whispered urgently, 'Come on, you big ox, don't just stand there farting in the wind – we've got work to do,' he decided he'd take the whore's remark as a compliment. Kissing her hand gallantly, he hissed into her ear, 'Remain true to me, my beloved. I shall return and then I shall demonstrate to you, my little cabbage, the full range of the tricks that my good German salami can perform.' And with that promise, he was scaling up the rough wall after the rest, to the flat roof where they were grouping, armed to the teeth, ready to break in.

Max and Schulze had drawn up the rescue plan together. Max, who had spent many a night, on account of drunkenness or similar petty crimes, in the place's cells, knew the prison intimately. He had pointed out right from the start that any attempt to go through the front entrance would result in severe casualties for the rescuers. The 'screws', as he called them, had a machine-gun post sited in the long tunnel which connected the outer and inner entrances to the cells. 'If the screws are not drunk, as they usually are, they'll slaughter us.'

Schulze had countered easily, 'Well, Max, if we can't go through the front entrance, as the lady said, we'll have to do it through the back one.' That had not proved possible, and in the end it had been Matz who had suggested the roof, 'Cos the Frogs won't expect us coming from that way, will they?'

It had been a suggestion they had all accepted at once and without question, especially as Max had pointed out, 'The screws reserve the upper-floor cells for the nutcases, you know.' He had tapped his right temple. 'For them suffering from the *cafard*. If there's any noise coming from that direction, the screws won't bother. There's always some poor mad swine up there minus all his cups in the cupboard, moaning and groaning and yelling his nut off.'

Now the twenty or so rescuers – the rest were positioned all around the barracks, ready for the escape – set about breaking in through the roof. It wasn't a difficult task. Like most buildings in that part of the world, the flat roof had been repaired many times, mostly very carelessly, and, working as they were by the fitful silver light of the sickle moon, as it scudded in and out of the clouds, they soon found less solid patches into which they could get their knives and crowbars and lever up the flags.

Now, as a clock in the Christian part of the town started to chime three, they were ready to enter the prison, each man armed in his own fashion – clubs, rubber truncheons, brass knuckles, knives – waiting for Max's signal. For, as he knew the prison layout so well, he would guide the party to where von Dodenburg was imprisoned.

In his cell on the second floor, Kuno tensed as the third stroke of the clock died away. It left a noisy silence, a buzzing in his ears which he knew was the result of tension. He was concerned, but not only for himself, also for his men. They were risking everything to save him, and he had no illusions about what action *Capitaine* Herresbach, the swine, would take if the rescue attempt failed. He'd have the lot of them shot out of hand.

But he knew he must not think of failure. The attempt would succeed, and he would ensure that he did whatever he could to help the plotters. Now, with his shoes muffled by the socks he had drawn over them, he crossed to the place where he had hidden the makeshift knife. In reality it was a razor-sharp sliver of metal he had levered from the inside of the evil-smelling piss bucket at the cost of severe lacerations and two painfully broken fingernails. The hilt of the sliver he had wrapped in his vest to protect his hand from any further damage. The weapon was primitive, very primitive indeed. But it would suffice to put any unsuspecting warder out of action, if he attempted to keep him in the cell.

Now he stationed himself behind the door, straining his ears for the first suspicious sound of his rescuers, his hand gripping the makeshift knife, suddenly damp with perspiration, a nerve ticking electrically at his temple. He started to count off the seconds, ready for the assault on the cell door. None came. 'Great crap on the Christmas tree,' he cursed to himself, full of impatience. 'Where in three devils are you, Schulze?'

At that moment, Sergeant Schulze was facing an emaciated prisoner of obviously German origin, for he spoke German, who was totally naked and was barring the way out of the third floor, repeating over and over again, 'You'll have to tickle me to get by, Adolf, come on now, tickle me, darling.' The madman grinned, revealing in the poor yellow light of the single electric bulb of the corridor a mouthful of smashed and blackened teeth. Again he gave a kind of hop-and-skip dance, raising the dust of the floor as he did so, and repeated the formula, 'You'll have to tickle me, Adolf . . . come on now, tickle me, darling.' This time he blew a frustrated Schulze a wet kiss.

That did it. Schulze could wait no longer. 'Come on,' he snarled. 'Come and be tickled, darling.'

The crazy man's faded eyes lit up. 'Do you mean it? Oh, I haven't been tickled for years now. Honest? You mean it?'

Schulze nodded. 'Yes, I do,' he answered, clubbing a fist like a small steam hammer. 'Come on, be tickled.'

As soon as the crazy man came within striking range, Schulze hit him, not particularly hard, but hard enough, straight on the point of his jaw. He went down as if poleaxed, with Matz catching him before he hit the ground, to lower him gently to the floor, saying as he did so, 'Poor old soldier. Doesn't even get killed.'

'Me heart bleeds,' Schulze said unfeelingly. Next moment he'd stepped over the crazy man and was heading for the door that led out of the third floor and away from its crazies.

Now things moved swiftly. A couple of sleepy warders were discovered, heads bent wearily over their cards. They were dealt with quickly. Another was found in the latrine. He was pushed backwards and sank into the thunderbox, bubbling and puffing mightily as he disappeared into the yellow horror. 'Don't bother, mate, you don't need to write,' Schulze chortled happily, and then he and Max were heading for von Dodenburg's cell, fumbling with the keys they had taken from the unfortunate warder. They'd almost done it, without a single casualty . . .

Herresbach woke with a start. Instinctively he knew something was going on. In the bed with him, the boy said something in his half-sleep, and his soft hand reached for the captain's genitals. Herresbach pushed the importuning fingers away. There seemed no time for that now. He shook his head and everything came into focus. At this remote border station, there was no 'dim-out'. But it seemed to him, as he glanced towards the window of his quarters, that there were more lights than usual. He flashed a glance at the green-glowing dial of his wristwatch. It was just past three in the morning. Who would be making so much light at this time of the day, he asked himself. Certainly not the local native merchants, who were the only ones who possessed electric light.

He sat abruptly. Next to him, the boy turned, stretched his naked body, and fell into a deep, probably dreamless sleep immediately. For a moment, Herresbach was tempted to forget

171

the mystery of the lights and snuggle up to him. Now the boy was nubile and sexually very attractive to him. A year or so more and his voice would break, he would grow hair and probably pimples too. Then he would be completely unattractive and then he, Herresbach, would have to find a replacement. It wasn't always easy to find the right kind of handsome boy, whom he could train to his peculiar ways and tastes.

He pricked up his ears. Over at the barracks, just beyond the prison, someone was attempting to start the reluctant engine of one of the regiment's trucks. He could just make out the harsh whirr of the starter handle and throaty choking gasps of an engine stubbornly refusing to fire. '*Himmel, Arsch und Wolkenbruch,*' he cursed, using German as he always did when he talked to himself. Something strange was going on. There was no early morning exercise planned for the regiment, and any messenger heading for headquarters in Damascus wouldn't use a truck; he'd use a motorcycle or a light vehicle – they were more economical.

His mind made up, the naked officer swung himself out of the rumpled bed. In a matter of seconds he was dressed, complete with his white kepi. Then, as an afterthought, he strapped on his revolver and strode out purposefully, flashing a last look at the handsome boy sleeping peacefully on his pillow. Then he was gone into the cool darkness. He'd never see the boy again.

Schulze laughed uproariously. The warder looked up at the giant who seemed to have appeared out of nowhere, pistol trembling in his pudgy hand. '*Que tu veux?*' he asked in a weak voice, still fumbling with the pistol.

Schulze didn't seem to notice the pistol. Instead he bellowed, 'Hold it there, you asparagus Tarzan.' The Frenchman didn't understand the German, but he did understand what happened next. Schulze's big foot lashed out. It caught the warder on his right shin. He yelped with pain. The pistol fell from his trembling hand and he bent over. Up came Schulze's knee. It caught him directly under his nostrils. The nose burst immediately under the impact of that tremendous blow. Blood and gore squirted everywhere, as the bone snapped, the Frenchman reeling back to slam against the concrete wall.

'*Los!*' Schulze cried. 'The CO must be here somewhere.'

Together in a mad scramble, the mixture of Wotan troopers and Legionnaires rushed down the dim passage. A warder poked his head out of a side room, saw the human avalanche descending upon him and fled back inside again. Then Schulze heard that familiar voice. '*Zu mir, Wotan!*' he yelled with all his strength, his pale haughty face contorted with a mixture of pride and gratitude. '*Hier!*'

One minute later, half a dozen hefty troopers were battering on his cell door as if their very lives depended upon it. Two minutes after that, they were freeing their beloved CO and hurrying down the corridor, heading for freedom and the trucks that should be waiting for them by now.

Two

Herresbach realized immediately what was happening. There had been some sort of mutiny in the Legion barracks, he guessed. The mutineers were now busy preparing the Panhard and Citroën trucks and half-tracks in the motor pool to flee. At the same time, he could tell from the blaze of lights over at the prison that something was going on over there, too.

Naturally, it was all the fault of those damned Germans of the SS, who had been interned in the Legion barracks. Probably they had suborned those Legionnaires who were of German origin. At all events, there was a small-scale mutiny taking place, and for a moment or two he was at a loss how to deal with it . . . Where were all the Legion's French officers? Had the mutineers killed them or confined them to their quarters? Herresbach knew that without their officers, the rest of the non-German Legionnaires wouldn't move into action against their fellow soldiers. Only their French officers could make them take up arms.

For a few minutes, revolver in hand, the captain stood there perplexed. Naturally the Germans could not be allowed to get away with this disgraceful mutiny, and for the moment he seemed unable to do anything here. Of course, he could call GHQ in Damascus. But the High Command, which was actively collaborating with France's enemy of a year before, would not permit any armed action against the Germans, especially as they had the German Control Commission looking over their shoulder in the Syrian capital.

Suddenly he had it. Without any one of standing to lead them, the mutiny would collapse as soon as it had started.

Most common soldiers were like dumb sheep, merely following the 'lead sheep'. And Herresbach knew that the 'lead sheep' in this remote frontier town was that arrogant swine Captain von Dodenburg. Deal with him nice and discreetly and the whole rotten mess would be cleared up in a flash.

His face hardened. Indeed, it would give him the greatest of pleasure to deal with the German swine, arrogant pig that he was, personally. But how was he going to do it?

The chatter of an old-fashioned machine gun, sounding like the noise of an irate woodpecker, cut into his reverie. He recognized the sound immediately. It was one of the handful of First World War machine guns with which the prison was equipped, and he knew this particular one was located between the inner and outer entrances to the prison. Obviously some of the warders were free and attempting to stop the break-out.

Herresbach hesitated no longer. Crouched low, so as to make the smallest possible target, he ran surprisingly quickly for such a big heavy man towards the main entrance of the prison. Now, as he got closer, he could hear the muffled shouts and cries from behind the thick walls, mixed with the slow chatter of the machine gun and the whine of the slugs howling off the concrete.

A woman was crouched there. What she was doing there, he neither knew nor cared. He hit her hard. She slammed to the wall and fell to the ground, unconscious before she hit it. He grunted and sucked his bruised knuckles before hurrying on. A dead warder lay sprawled across the main entrance, stretched out in the extravagant posture of one done violently to death. He sprang over the body. Standing with his back to the door, he gave it a slight kick. It opened wider. He flashed a glance inside. Up in the inner darkness of the connecting corridor, there were the angry, violent flashes of a machine gun firing in the direction of the prison's interior. He hesitated no longer. He started to run down the corridor to where the gun crew were squatting. A corporal in charge heard the echoing footsteps. He swung round and recognized the captain. 'Sheer hell, sir,' he gasped, the blood trickling down the side of his face from a scalp wound. 'But we're holding them – *just*. But all they've got to do is to wait for a stoppage, or while we change the belt, and they'll rush us.'

'I understand.' Herresbach brushed aside the explanation sharply. 'I want to get in . . . but not to face that mob in there.'

The corporal looked shocked, as if the big captain had suddenly gone mad, but he knew Herresbach's reputation, so he didn't argue. 'Over to the right, sir.' He indicated a little door in the side wall. 'Up the stairs and you're on top of the inner wall, then—' But Herresbach was already gone, slipping through the small door and mounting the winding stair that led to the wall and the interior of the prison.

Now the attackers had gone to ground in the face of the heavy machine-gun fire coming from the outer corridor. 'Shit on the shingle!' Schulze cursed as he lay there with a stream of tracer cutting the air just above his head. 'Why the frig didn't I take that into account?' He meant the machine gun. 'A single grenade and I'd have blown the Frog perverts to hell tootsweet.'

Under other circumstances, von Dodenburg would have been amused at Schulze's anger, but not now. So far everything had gone smoothly. Now this single machine gun was holding up the whole escape, and he guessed they didn't have much time left. The alarm would sound and then they'd probably face the full strength of the Vichy French Army in Syria. He had to do something and he had to do it damned fast. But what?

It was Max, the big red-bearded ex-communist, who came up with the answer. 'Sir.' He addressed von Dodenburg as if he were already part of Wotan's First Company.

'Yes?'

'We used Schulze here as a human bridge to get inside this place, sir.'

'Yes, you frigging well did,' Schulze agreed darkly. 'And frigging well nearly ruined my sex life doing so.'

Max ignored the NCO. 'Well, we could use the same dodge to get outside of it. At least, some of us could. If we can get behind them and catch them off guard . . .' He didn't finish his sentence; instead he clasped and twisted his huge hairy paws together, as if he were choking the life out of one of the warders.

Von Dodenburg didn't hesitate. He knew he hadn't the time. 'Let's use the dead ground over there – right, see it?' he said urgently. Schulze opened his mouth to protest, but in the garish red light cast by the machine gun firing all out, he could see that it wouldn't be of any use. He let his shoulders sink in defeat.

Von Dodenburg started to crawl towards the wall. Immediately the French gunner turned his weapon on the crawling man. Slugs slapped into the cobbles on both sides of von Dodenburg, chips of stone cut his face. He kept going. A few steps and he'd be in dead ground. The French gunner must have known it, too. He loosed another volley at the crawling man. Even in the darkness, von Dodenburg could see the bullets coming ever closer, striking up little flashes of violent light as they struck the ground. In the very last moment, a desperate von Dodenburg gave a kind of leap forward and the bullets were cutting the air behind him harmlessly. He had done it.

For a moment or two he rested there, trying to contain his heavy breathing. Then he was in charge of himself, his breathing under control, his hands steady. He touched the wall. It was made up of rough-hewn stones. There were plenty of handholds. Even in the darkness he'd manage it. He spat on his palms like some labourer about to start a hard day's work, and grabbed the first handhold. Moments later he was on his way upwards. Behind him Schulze cursed angrily once again and told himself he shouldn't have let the CO go it alone. But now it was too late. So he turned to the others lying on the cobbles behind him and cried above the chatter of the machine gun, 'Once the CO nobbles the Frog popgun, move, and move frigging fast. Time's running out. Clear?'

There was a murmur of agreement, though Matz was only one of those who at that moment doubted whether von Dodenburg could 'nobble the Frog popgun' so easily. But he kept that thought to himself.

Panting a little, von Dodenburg swung himself over the parapet and crouched there in the glowing darkness, listening to the attempts of the rest of Schulze's party trying to start the trucks over at the barracks. By now in the border city there was noise everywhere as the inhabitants became aware, too, that something strange was going on at the barracks and the prison. He guessed it wouldn't be long before the authorities realized that something was wrong and started to take action. It was imperative that he should silence that damned machine gun so that they could get out and be on their way before the real balloon went up.

His breathing calmer now, he set off again, feeling his way along the wall, trying to find some way of getting down to the rear of the machine gun down below. Once he thought he'd found a door that opened up to a passage leading to the ground. But it proved to be locked or bricked up and, cursing under his breath, he was forced to continue, groping his way along the wall in the darkness.

It was when he was about ready to give up in despair that he felt the cooler air strike him in the face, air heavy with the stink of cat's piss and ancient prison misery. Immediately he realized that there was an opening somewhere close at hand. His heart leapt. This was it! He pushed forward and then stopped dead. Enclosed in a doorway, looking like a statue, let into the wall of some medieval Gothic church, there was a silent figure staring at him. For a moment he felt the small hairs at the back of his head stand erect with the shock. Who was this ghostly figure waiting for him thus?

Next moment he knew as that well-remembered voice said in his thick Alsatian dialect, 'Well, the man I want to meet. *Hauptsturmführer* von Dodenburg personally.'

'Herresbach!' Kuno retorted, shocked. 'You?'

'Exactly. Who had you expected? Father Christmas, perhaps.'

'*Arschloch!*' von Dodenburg cried, and started to move forward.

He stopped the very next instant as Herresbach commanded, 'Stay there, if you want to live a little longer.'

There was enough authority – and menace – in Herresbach's voice to make him stop. He guessed the French officer would be armed, and all he'd got was the crude home-made knife. What was he to do? He knew he could expect no mercy from Herresbach. Still, he had to do something. If he didn't, Schulze, Matz and all the rest who had rescued him would suffer, perhaps even with their lives. He took another pace forward. 'I said – stay there,' Herresbach's harsh voice commanded once more. Herresbach felt at the back of his belt for his revolver. He drew it out of its holster and clicked off the safety catch.

Kuno couldn't see him exactly in the darkness, but he knew what that sharp metallic click signified. Herresbach was armed, and sooner or later he was going to use his weapon. The Alsatian would show no mercy. It was clear what he had to do – it was a matter of kill or be killed.

'Step forward – *slowly*,' he heard Herresbach say, as if he were speaking from a long way off. 'Raise your hands.'

Von Dodenburg hesitated for a moment. He made a swift movement with his right hand. He raised both hands then and moved forward, body held rigid, waiting for the first hard impact of Herresbach's bullet. He didn't trust the Alsatian. The latter had no concept of honour between officers or the rules of war.

Now he could make out Herresbach more clearly. He had stepped out of the dark framework of the door. In his right hand he held his revolver, levelled straight at him. And Herresbach was grinning, showing his big yellow tomb-like teeth in triumph. He thought he had all the aces in his hand, von Dodenburg could tell that. He was going to enjoy this moment of victory, savour every last second of it.

Herresbach said: 'You thought you were damned clever, von Dodenburg, didn't you? You Germans always do. Making traitors of our troops, just as you have done with that dirty pack of collaborators back in France.' He laughed. 'This time you picked the wrong man to play your supposed clever tricks on.'

'At least I'm not a goddam pervert like you, Herresbach,' von Dodenburg needled him suddenly. He reasoned that if he taunted the other man, he might lose control of himself. 'I am

179

an honest soldier. I have no truck with perverted little boys, like you do.'

'*Sale cochon!*' Herresbach cursed. He pulled the trigger in the same instant that von Dodenburg launched himself forward. Kuno yelled with pain. What felt like a red-hot poker plunged deep into his right leg. Next moment he slammed into Herresbach with all his weight. The other man was caught off balance. He staggered against the wall, just above the steps leading down below to where the machine-gun team was. Desperately he attempted to regain his balance, lashing out at von Dodenburg's pain-contorted face with the muzzle of his pistol.

Kuno felt himself blacking out with the agony of his leg. But he wouldn't let himself go under. Vaguely he heard the corporal below cry, '*Le Capitaine – il est blessé!*' The chatter of the machine gun ceased. Kuno didn't wait for it to start again. He ripped the makeshift knife from left to right across Herresbach's hard stomach, trying to find a spot where he could plunge the knife in deep. There it was, just below the other man's belly button. He waited no longer. 'Try that on for size, you perverted swine!' he cried, and with the last of his strength plunged the knife in deep.

Herresbach grunted like a stuck pig. His back arched like a taut bowstring. He hit Kuno across the face with his pistol muzzle once more. This time the blow was weaker; Kuno hardly felt it. But he was blacking out fast. 'Die . . . you bastard – *die!*' he hissed, and slipped the knife in once more. He felt the hot blood flood his right hand. He ripped the knife upwards with the last of his failing strength, the black veil descending before his eyes. The blade snapped. Herresbach whispered something and then the two of them, locked together like passionate lovers in one final embrace, tumbled down the stairs and, from below, Schulze was yelling at the top of his voice, 'Up the wall, you dogs. Come on, crack your nuts . . . up the frigging wall and help the CO.'

That was the last Kuno von Dodenburg heard as Herresbach died slowly.

Envoi

The Führer laughed. As always, he felt at ease with his paladins of the SS, especially those from his own body-guard regiment, *die Leibstandarte*. They were all there, the senior members, the juniors, even a few favoured NCOs who had won decorations in the regiment's last two years of campaigning in Europe. There was Sepp Dietrich, Keitel, his chief of staff, of course, then the younger ones, Peiper, Bremer, Frey, who would all be generals if the war lasted long enough – and they survived in one piece.

Standing on the sidelines, von Dodenburg, face still pale from his month in hospital in Athens, leaning on his stick for support, envied them, as did his chief, the Vulture. For Wotan wasn't going in the first wave of the great attack, as was the *Leibstandarte*. Wotan hadn't recovered yet from its ordeal and losses in Iraq. Indeed, they were still waiting for reinforce-ments from the Reich. But, as the Führer had assured the two officers immediately after his arrival at this new front-to-be, 'Never fear, my dear Colonel Geier – and you, too, von Dodenburg, SS Wotan will see action soon enough. I can always use my heroes of the Führer's Fire Brigade!' Hitler had laughed, and for one dreadful moment, he thought the leader was about to pinch his cheek, as he was wont to do with his teenage SS men.

'When this attack starts,' Hitler was saying to the *Leibstandarte* officers, 'you can take it from me, gentlemen, the world will hold its breath and tremble. For then our friends and our foes will realize that we can take on the world, if necessary, and beat it. So we made a mistake in Iraq. But it was only a minor one, and our allies weren't as efficient as we expected them to be. Now, however, for the time being we are on our own – and we shall still achieve our aim and make the world tremble at the power of German arms.' He stamped his foot down and clenched his fists in an upward movement, as if he were doing some kind of peasant jig.

The Vulture sniffed at the words, but said nothing. Neither did von Dodenburg. Instead he was thinking of all those dead young Germans who had left their bones to bleach in the Iraq wastes for no important purpose. What use had it all been? The English had triumphed in the end; they were in control once more, and what had been left of Wotan had only escaped by the skin of their teeth, a bunch of hunted fugitives, racked by injuries and sickness. Now, on this June morning in 1941, as Hitler prepared to attack across the River Bug into Russia, all they were capable of, militarily, was to act as a flank guard to the *Leibstandarte*. 'How are the mighty fallen . . .' he commented bitterly to no one in particular.

The Vulture turned and peered at him through his monocle, as if he were seeing the younger man for the first time. 'Once the gentlemen of the *Leibstandarte* start taking serious casualties, von Dodenburg, they'll need us. We can provide the cannon fodder for the Führer's favourites. Then they – and the Führer, too – will realize the worth of SS Assault Battalion Wotan.'

Von Dodenburg was appalled by the Vulture's callous attitude. Was that all the men of Wotan – perhaps, now 'boys' would be a better description – were worth? Cannon fodder, dying merely to bring Wotan, and naturally the Vulture, to the attention of the military authorities? He opened his mouth to protest, but then thought better of it. He knew the Vulture of old. Instead he raised his night glasses and focused them on the enemy side of the river. Nothing seemed to move there. No smoke came from the thatched little Russian cottages, the *isbas*. Not even a dog howled at the night shadows. For all that, von Dodenburg could see the whole countryside over there might well be totally devoid of human life.

But he knew he was wrong. There were people out there, perhaps already awake and just waiting for them to come in their stormboats to be mown down in their hundreds, thousands. He shivered suddenly. 'A louse ran over your liver?' the Vulture queried, without interest.

'Something like that, sir,' he answered.

'Don't worry, von Dodenburg, we'll go through them like shit through a goose.'

''Spect so, sir,' he answered the CO without conviction.

Now there was movement to their immediate front. The staff was seeing the Führer off before the battle commenced. No one wanted to have a dead Hitler on his conscience; he wouldn't live long anyway, if anything happened to the Leader. There was a clicking of heels. Arms went up rigidly. Hard voices cried, 'Heil Hitler!' The Führer was on his way back to the safety of his headquarters.

Von Dodenburg raised his arm in the Hitler greeting without enthusiasm. It wasn't just his wound. It was really a feeling of let-down. He had been here before, Poland on 31st August, 1939; Holland on 10th May 1940 . . . All those beginnings over the last two years, when excitement had run high, as the tanks massed, the artillery swung into position and the infantry readied to march. What hopes they all had had. Naturally there had been victories, deeds of great daring, medals, honours. But each time the cost in human life had seemed higher, and in the end the great victories seemed to have solved nothing. Now, this dawn of June 22nd 1941, they were fighting once more, against perhaps the strongest enemy of all, Soviet Russia. But would a victory in this enormous country bring a final peace and a stop to the slaughter? Von Dodenburg, a puzzled young man, didn't know.

A kilometre or so away, well camouflaged in his hide, not far from the Russian first line of defence, another young man, dark-skinned and handsome, dressed in a uniform with the green stripes of the NKVD[*], lowered his night glasses too. Ever since he had been first sent to Germany as a teenager of wealthy Indian parents, he had been fighting fascism for the cause of the Soviet Fatherland. Now, as he surveyed the SS fascists, whom he had almost led into a trap only weeks

[*] Russian Secret Police/Secret Service.

before, he was convinced that this time they wouldn't escape. This time they were doomed. Satisfied that he had done all he could for the time being, the one-time Lieutenant Singh of the 'Indian Legion' crept out of his hide to the waiting motorbike that would take him back to Army HQ.

Sergeant Schulze, cleaning the dirt out from under his toenails with the point of his bayonet, commented to his equally glum running mate, the 'Bavarian barnshitter', *'Buy combs, lads . . . there's lousy times ahead . . .'*